ANALOG DAYS

ALSO IN THE NVLA SERIES

The Plotinus
RIKKI DUCORNET

We're Safe When We're Alone
NGHIEM TRAN

Cecilia
K-MING CHANG

Sound Museum
POUPEH MISSAGHI

Patchwork
TOM COMITTA

ANALOG DAYS

Damion Searls

COFFEE HOUSE PRESS
Minneapolis
2025

Copyright © 2025 by Damion Searls
Cover design by Sarah Evenson
Book design by Rachel Holscher
Author photo © 2025 by Beowulf Sheehan

Coffee House Press books are available to the trade through our primary distributor, Consortium Book Sales & Distribution, cbsd.com or (800) 283-3572. For personal orders, catalogs, or other information, write to info@coffeehousepress.org.

Coffee House Press is a nonprofit literary publishing house. Support from private foundations, corporate giving programs, government programs, and generous individuals helps make the publication of our books possible. We gratefully acknowledge their support in detail in the back of this book.

All rights reserved. No part of this book may be used or reproduced in any manner for the purpose of training artificial intelligence technologies or systems.

LIBRARY OF CONGRESS CATALOGING-IN PUBLICATION DATA

Names: Searls, Damion author.
Title: Analog days / Damion Searls.
Description: Minneapolis : Coffee House Press, 2025.
Identifiers: LCCN 2025013339 (print) | LCCN 2025013340 (ebook) | ISBN 9781566897396 paperback | ISBN 9781566897402 epub
Subjects: LCGFT: Novellas
Classification: LCC PS3619.E2559 A84 2025 (print) | LCC PS3619.E2559 (ebook) | DDC 813/.6—dc23/eng/20250408
LC record available at https://lccn.loc.gov/2025013339
LC ebook record available at https://lccn.loc.gov/2025013340

PRINTED IN THE UNITED STATES OF AMERICA

32 31 30 29 28 27 26 25   1 2 3 4 5 6 7 8

The NVLA series is an artistic playground where authors challenge and broaden the outer edges of storytelling. Each novella illuminates the capacious and often overlooked space of possibilities between short stories and novels. Unified by Sarah Evenson's bold and expressive series design, NVLA places works as compact as they are complex in conversation to demonstrate the infinite potential of the form.

ANALOG DAYS

Every generation has its memories.
—*Joseph Conrad*

This is something that happened before it all started: My Berkeley friend offered me her ex-fiancé's old car. You try to go back to the beginning but when you do there's still everything before the beginning, and what about that? All sorts of things keep happening, as the history books say: some of them good, some of them bad.

The ex-fiancé had wanted to learn Arabic and gone to the language institute in Monterey, he couldn't afford to study it otherwise. Accordion player, Dylan fan. He would never have to serve. That was pre-2001. Now it was after and he was off to Iraq and decided to drive across the country to where he had to report for duty. After a breakdown (not automotive, mental), he left his car in Boulder, flew to Georgia. The car was mine if I wanted it.

A strange letter came in the mail, sealed with black duct tape and written in crazy-looking capital letters. It was a handwritten deed on the back of a page of Arabic language exercises.

I called the Colorado number I had and spoke to an old man who said yeah, it's on the lawn, come'n get it. I had pictured a Toyota or Honda for some reason; it was a brown Ford Bronco, the old kind.

The whole thing started to feel too weird.

I didn't call back or go get the truck. Someone I didn't know had had a breakdown in it and was off to the war in Iraq and it just didn't seem worth it.

I asked my friend every now and then about her ex-fiancé. She said she got emails saying if she knew what he was doing she would never speak to him again. Then I started seeing the pictures from Abu Ghraib, and imagined the duties of an Arabic translator, and was glad not to have his Ford Bronco. I wondered if, technically, I owned it, the deed was still in a drawer somewhere, I thought, but I've packed and moved across the country since and never saw it.

Someone finally went on TV, wrote editorials, about what he had done at Abu Ghraib and why and who had told him to. Finally someone said it. He became one of my heroes, pretty much all we had in that terrible year. It took a while before I made the connection and realized that it's his car I could have owned, or maybe do own. I pictured driving around in it sometimes, in my mind, listening to Dylan. One of the dark albums, the ones about America. *Blood on the Tracks, Bringing It All Back Home.* I guess really they're all dark.

Passing through the Bay Area again not too long ago I found myself at the San Francisco Public Library trying to track down a shadowy recording studio. I would have to say that's when it started.

JUNE 21, 2016   TUESDAY

The downtown New York bar had a hidden back room, and out the back of that the shallowest courtyard any of us had ever seen. A strip of tables and Russian-looking birch trees on a narrow twin bed of yellow leaves. No sooner out the sliding door you were face to face with a crumbly stone wall, grayish white. Both ends of the courtyard are even more claustrophobic, blocked in by the high backs of buildings; narrow alleys, barely room for a bike, run out around the bar to the street. The gray-white wall, though close, and at least ten or twelve feet high, is lower than the buildings, and almost soft—the color, the texture—and is comforting, not crowding.

The whole gang was there: Pam and Chris, Edward, Jennifer, Gideon, Josh and Ben, Scott, Anne-Sofie, Iris, Jeon.

Where's John, Pam said.

The chronicler, she said.

Still in San Francisco, Scott said.

Jennifer was talking about her date, David, teacher (sexy), smart. They'd been waiting for their drinks when the man at the next table had started talking to David.

Can I tell you my philosophical idea?

Okay . . . , David had said.

What is truth?

That's not an idea, that's a question!

Ha ha, okay. What is truth?

What do you think truth is.

Analog Days   3

I think: Truth is that which does not change.

Pause. I guess I don't really agree with that, David said.

Let me put it this way, the man at the next table said, having obviously put it this way many times. If something is here today gone tomorrow can it be the truth?

Some kinds of truth are like that, some aren't. Are you only talking about religious truth?

God is truth.

Yes, if you believe in God then I see how you could say truth doesn't change. But not everyone believes in God.

I do believe in God.

But then other people have different ideas of truth.

If something changes, can it be the truth?

David was trying to engage the man, in his way, Jennifer said, but the man couldn't have the conversation David wanted to have. Though David couldn't have the conversation the man wanted to have either. I liked him for trying, for taking the man seriously.

The man's wife, also sitting at the next table, was smiling uncomfortably, having been through this before. She had a weasel face, but not in a bad way, Jennifer said: small round head, sharp features, smart and sly, all sorts of fascinating thoughts to share if she chose to. Perched on her nose were enormous bright white Buddy Holly glasses like a heron on a low gable. See what I mean?

Well, Jennifer said David went on, there's political truths, or social truths. Thirty years ago it was impossible to elect a black president in this country, that was a real truth, and now we have a black president. A truth about our society has changed.

That's not the truth.

Why not? Which part's false?

I knew right then that I would never love this man, Jennifer said. He couldn't go with the situation—couldn't speak this stranger's language. He was rigid in just the way he thought he was arguing against. And he had forgotten about me.

It was six o'clock. Something always happens at six, Scott quoted. Chris got up to get more drinks.

A craggy-faced barman behind the counter was polishing a tumbler with a gray cloth. To two unacquainted men on barstools who'd just ordered the same drink he said, with a twinkle: You fellows been together long? Chris came back and told everyone.

Then he announced: One of the things people don't realize is also there during the long philosophical conversations in movies is the background noise. Visual noise too. You can zone out and notice the reflections in the mirror, the song on the jukebox, the face of the bartender. Having something else to pay attention to lets you follow the conversation better.

I saw this movie once, Josh said. It was supposed to be about history and memory, but the billboard for *Jaws* in the background gave more reality than anything else in the film.

It's weird, typewriters on desks don't do it as much as giant word-processor monitors.

Puffy sleeves!

Cordless landlines!

Right, but whatever a writer tries to put in as period detail feels fake, or like trying too hard, Chris went on. You need the invisible detail, the filler—what we don't notice, don't see. Collars, hairdos. Film can do it, writing can't.

Our group does more than trade stories and images, but the rest doesn't matter that much to be honest. Someone once told us we all sounded the same when we talked; we took it as a compliment.

Please forgive these digressions.—

JUNE 22, 2016   WEDNESDAY

Governor Doug Ducey of Arizona declares a state of emergency in Navajo County, where fires fueled by record-shattering heat have engulfed more than 40,000 acres.

Great Britain continues to mourn MP Jo Cox, stabbed and shot to death last Thursday on the first anniversary of white supremacist Dylann Roof's marauding at the Emanuel Church in Charleston. Jo Cox had been 41, a mother of two, known for her passionate support for Syrian refugees and a vocal advocate for Britain to stay in the EU. She was the first member of the British Parliament to be murdered in more than twenty-five years. During the attack, eyewitnesses said, her killer shouted "Britain First," the name of a far-right anti-immigrant political party; he is a longtime supporter of the neo-Nazi National Alliance and stated his name in court as Death To Traitors, Freedom For Britain. The Brexit vote is tomorrow.

I remember a middle-aged man watching the light, alone on a park bench in the rain. The umbrella's fabric sits right on his head, more for convenience one might say than to keep him dry; he leans forward a bit, putting his head and back closer to his knees and feet, but he can still feel the ring of rain coming down on much of his body while he watches his son stomp in puddles and rocket off the end of the wet fast slide. Early one early May morning,—trees pale green and full, sky overcast, the light somehow clean, even in the city. More things than usual seemed possible.

In the US parliament, eight days after the deadliest mass shooting in American history, while victims' families watch from seats around the senate chamber, senators vote today that people on the federal terrorism watchlist should still be able to buy guns, and that background check loopholes should still not be closed. Four gun-control measures fail, none of which in any case would have banned the AR-15 semiautomatic assault rifle used in Orlando, in San Bernardino, in Aurora, in Sandy Hook Elementary School.

That May morning I must have been back in New York for two years. I'd moved in the spring. There was work for me as a coder, enough to make it as a freelancer.

Without working seventy-hour weekends I would never get far, but it would do. I'd left New York for a while but never left New York. Here we come to the heart of the matter, I would say: I have never left the houses, the streets, the neighborhoods where I grew up.

Back where I'd grown up, what rose up were images. A huge medallion of paper flowers on the half-wall high behind the café counter—blue roses, sea green, orange, several different reds, in a large ring.

A white woman on the street—young, black hair, smoker type, New York armor loaded up (sunglasses, shoulder bag, scowl). On her t-shirt, in big sans-serif caps, black on off-white: I AM A / FUCKING / ZOMBIE.

The morning is cool, bright, and dry on the walk to the park. "And if you go broke, then ya go to Hellllll . . ." the black kid sings quietly, earbuds probably in his ears. The playground is sprinkled with white light. Later, school out, with half-naked children running around in the taut, intersecting jets of water from the three sprinklers.

The playground in my childhood memories is a large enclosure on several levels, starting on the north end with a large flat area of slides, seesaws, sandboxes, and swings surrounded by fences, bordered by green and often broken benches. In the playground from today the benches are fixed, the monkey bars new, and two large brown dinosaurs for climbing on or detouring around—not large for dinosaurs I suppose—rear up between the sandboxes. The children today, it is strange to think, will have memories as strong of those dinosaurs as I do of the space they now fill.

The barbell-shaped zone on the lower level opens out at the southern end into an arena enclosed in high walls, with a concentric circle inside ringed by a metal fence, the fountain, and from the southern edge of that circle steps lead up to memories of endless childhood handball and a mezzanine with benches, picnic tables. An attendant's shed there looks like a little castle, bathroom doors permanently locked, and more steps lead up from there to the highest level, joining with the park outside the playground. A long hill from the northern end of the playground leads up to that same flat promenade, with its view down to the river.

As a bike climbs that hillside under the high trees, let us reconstruct the memories of the time I went there so often. There are memories of the light, memories of the games, the sandbox scooping, the handball, the finding someone to seesaw with. Of being alone, and of groups: girls playing ring-around-the-rosy, one lonesome girl, crying, and the rest of us acting like we don't notice, which is surely the decent thing to do. There is Tamara, the girl with braids and flowers in her hair who climbed a tree at my eighth birthday party, and the bigger kid who played dodgeball with us, and threw the ball in my face on purpose, blood ran from my nose, I was surprised, and then—I don't remember the transition—we were friends. Matt and me and his four younger brothers, his parents were "going to keep trying till they got a girl or a baseball team," I remember, which only vaguely made sense to me, and I don't know which they ended up with, Matt moved away, probably to a cheaper neighborhood with bigger apartments. Priya, who lived down the block, and our endless turns on the seesaw. Hilary, Phoebe, and Aglaya playing jacks with a maraschino-red superball. And Sylvie, oh, Sylvie.

I hardly knew her, because I never dared to talk to her. Finally, yes, at that ring-around-the-rosy with the girls all singing and the crying girl in the middle, not her, we talked and we hid behind the bench near the sandbox. Such a surplus of thrilling, inflaming imprecisions life rests on. Later she had to sing a song to regain her place in the dance, which she did in a fresh young voice as the shadows came down from the great trees. The next time I saw her, we held hands. Maybe—I think now—she'd had a crush on me too that whole time. She was my age, old enough for early sorrow. She was moving away, Priya told me afterward, I never saw her again. Until last week.

JUNE 23, 2016   THURSDAY

Thunder and lightning—lightning flashes that seem to follow the rumbles of thunder instead of vice versa, so distant and frequent they come—but no rain. At last, huge black circles on the gray slate ledge and a loud crash and down it comes. It's still oppressively hot but

I open a window to hear it fall. The lightning comes faster, it seems to flash between me and the wall. The windows run wetly and blurrily; clouds of spray bounce off the roofs opposite. CD: Zorn, *Nosferatu*.

Yesterday, a mother and daughter on the train: mother black-with-white hair, not gray, big clunky euro-glasses, scarf mounded at the neck, dark burgundy lipstick on thin lips, olive skin, mannish face; daughter young with slicked-back dyed-brown hair, wearing black except for gray fake-fur fringe on her coat and black and white checked sneakers, almost waifish but too angular, and carrying an enormous camera. I thought they must be French; they were Dutch. The girl checked the view screen and fiddled with some settings, camera pointed down; I think she was pretending to review some shots she had already taken but the camera was aimed at my feet and it clicked a couple of times while she avoided eye contact. Maybe that was her strategy. Maybe my feet were more interesting than I thought that day, or it was a chance-based serial project.

I especially remember the pictures of my feet on the train because later that day I hurt my foot, tore a tendon, jumping down from a low wall in the park and landing on something spongy.—Somewhere on the wall of some art school in Nijmegen next end of semester there will probably be the last record of my undamaged feet.

I could still order deliveries of food and everything else I needed, of course. It made a lot of things simpler really.

Decide to think everything over twice, the day of and day after. Iris says Thoreau said to do that. Josh says Porphyry had his students lie silently in bed first thing every morning and revisit the previous day's events, what they'd done and what they'd learned. Time gets an overlapping texture, folds and thicknesses, or like tile roofs. Remember those long plastic rods with a hard flap for each letter, obsolete office equipment used to alphabetize index cards or name tags? When they're empty all the flaps point the same way on the desk. Waves on the beach of course, each one crashing and spilling over the last. Time foams and froths bright white. Jennifer sometimes says: "Thinking is more interesting than knowing."

JUNE 24, 2016   FRIDAY

Last night England and Wales voted to leave the European Union. David Cameron immediately announced his resignation as Prime Minister of the hitherto United Kingdom; Alexander Boris de Pfeffel Johnson is favored to succeed him.

"It would be horribly tragic if my ability to protect myself or my family were to be taken away, but that's exactly what Democrats are determined to do by banning semi-automatic handguns," prominent gun activist Christy Sheats of Fulshear, Texas, wrote recently on Facebook. Today she ends a family meeting by chasing her two daughters (Madison, 17; Taylor, 22) out the front door and shooting them dead. A Fulshear police officer shoots and kills her on the street after she refuses to drop her weapon.

At this moment suddenly appeared from nowhere the first of a long line of maleficent beings, Josh quoted. You could always tell when he was quoting, his voice got harder somehow, redder.

On the subway: John said, back in town, sitting with the group at the downtown bar, his foot in a big plastic boot: I was sitting across from a man about thirty, fleshy not fat, practicing cards. He shuffles with his right hand, then with his left; he fans out the cards, pulls out and turns over a single card from the middle of the pack, then snaps them all back into a neat pile, first with his right hand, then all with his left; he cuts, he palms, he cascades, all perfectly, with a terrible frown on his face, and that is the key to the image, a sad frown like a clown's, not moving a muscle in his face, lips reaching farther to the sides of his head than I've ever seen in a living person under sad eyes that never look down. He is sitting in one of the two-seat corner spots on the subway and I'm opposite him; the train is half full. I can't stop watching his magnificent hands. I'm sure he knows I'm looking but he never makes eye contact. He is manipulating the cards when I step in the train door and still at it when I leave, John said. Image.

It was a sound I noticed first, Gideon said, behind the noise of the train, a tapping and a clacking. Candy Crush to the left of me, texting to the right. I couldn't help looking: "i forgive u i really want the best for u and i am so sad and sorry that" and I turned my eyes away as her thumbs kept clacking, from the human drama on the right to the colored doodads on the left.

I used to be able to read on the sly in buses and trains: Gideon again now: other people's newspapers, book titles, a chapter heading or a page. It wasn't an invasion of their privacy. They were reading in public, the same way they talked or wore their clothes, a tacit agreement to see and be seen, hear and be heard. Now that they're writing breakup notes out in the world, it seems cruel to intrude, selfish, almost violent. Now it's my fault for looking. They've shattered the public, dispersed the aether. I used to love public life in New York, now I share it only with people sitting empty-handed or reading printed books. I never see newspapers anymore.—

It seems like it shouldn't matter to you if everyone around you is on a phone or a Kindle, but it does, Scott says.

Are you allowed to say this anymore? someone asks. That battle was lost ten years ago. I remember the same grumpy nonsense about how terrible the Walkman was, from thirty.

A street scene of Paris in a movie from fifty years ago is so different from today, Gideon says. It's not just the black-and-white, or the hats, or the lack of ads on every surface, wall, clothes, kiosk, bus stop. It's the presence, somehow. (He comes off better here.)

Neil Young, Jeon said, says he used to work out his songs live,—try things out onstage, see what works. But now that everything's put up on YouTube that means putting underdone music out there, and then next time everyone says he doesn't know his own songs. So it all has to be worked out in advance. A form of life, of artistic practice, that required the presence of other people is no longer possible; the audience is no longer able to be there as people, only devices, recording and comparing.

Do you remember where you were when the internet first let you down? I bet you do. This was Mark, a writer, pretty well-known at least in Brooklyn—Mark Slope, you've seen the t-shirts.

It's like where they were when they heard Kennedy was shot, but for us. I don't mean the first mistake you found on Wikipedia or crazy comment, but the first time the whole thing failed you: the kind of information that has to be online, that doesn't exist if it isn't on the web, just wasn't there. If you're of a certain age, your faith in the internet was learned—a savvy friend had to show you Netscape 1.0 and all the different search engines—Alta Vista; Northern Lights; Ask Jeeves—and had to tell you No, really, this is going to be huge, even though to you it all seemed slow and pointless. Eventually you learned it. You *could* buy a plane ticket, sometimes even the first class to Europe for twenty dollars glitch, it wasn't an urban legend, I found one myself one shining day. You could ask and Jeeves could answer; soon Google knew everything. You didn't grow up believing in the web, you had to bring yourself around. Maybe that makes its failure all the more painful.

Analog Days 15

On my last day of college, John says, when I was moving out of the dorm, there were these official-looking notes in everyone's mailbox: The university was "getting" something called "electronic-mail" and here were our "addresses." I didn't know what they were talking about and I crumpled up the paper and threw it away in a garbage can already filled to the top with yellow notes—I was moving in with a friend anyway, and didn't know what my address would be in a few months. That was my Commencement.

It's not like now, when everyone's disappointed, Mark says.

Mark is obsessed with trying to get off the web completely. For a while he was trying to find a publisher for the world's first print blog. He called it a plog. The same way blogs are not just uploaded diaries or short essays—maybe they were at first, but then they became a new kind of writing—so, too, the plog is not just a printout of blog entries but a form of its own, Mark would tell whoever would listen. Some might argue, he said, that every column or miscellany before 1994 was a plog, but no: It means something different to walk or bike across the country after cars and planes; it means something different to mail a letter now that there's email; so too writing. If everything about how the web changes the way we think has any truth, then print vs. plog makes a difference.

He tried to go radical, life-writing without the internet—no writing about books bought from Amazon or ABE, no fact-checking on Wikipedia, no news of the world from the world-wide web. When he traveled somewhere to plog about it, he bought his ticket in person at a travel agent's actual office, or over the phone, calling a number he'd found in a paper phone book or a posted ad he'd seen on the street.

We pointed out that the agent used the internet to book his ticket, the plane itself was fully digital, etc.,—there's no way to go analog alone,—but he said it was meant as a record of his offline life insofar as it's possible to still have one, or have had one. Unlike before, he said, I bear the weight of my sense that everything is not inaccessible—it is right at my fingertips and I am choosing not to click on it. Logistical difficulties have become moral.

He couldn't get the plog published, of course. Newspapers don't serialize; magazines would never take it; anything too ziney and cliquey couldn't even pretend to be reaching a public. He considered photocopying leaflets and handing them out. People kept telling him to publish it online, which was the one way he couldn't, that was the whole point. Finally he thought that, though it wasn't ideal, a book could still get the serial feel if it was designed right.

He was well connected enough to have a lunch with a New York editor;—he told us about it that night, under the birch trees. The editor had talked about "platform."

What's that? John had asked, he was not a writer.

A publisher, Mark said, needs to know why *you* are the person who can write this book, and sell it. Celebrities automatically have a platform; maybe you have a popular blog, or teach at Harvard on the topic, or are the biography subject's estranged daughter. What matters is your platform, not your idea or your writing.

Platform? Mark had cried. My platform is the Imagination!

The editor politely informed me, Mark had said, that in that case the books I wrote would be published in the imagination too. I quoted: Men think they can Copy Nature as Correctly as I copy Imagination this they will find Impossible! The editor said that was nice and that he was only trying to help and he called for the check.

Now Mark runs unplugged field trips. People pay him to walk them around a neighborhood and encourage them to talk or daydream and forbid them from taking out their phones. He calls these outings analog days. We don't see him as much as the rest of the group, but he doesn't seem to mind not hearing about things. When he's in the mood we get phone calls from his landline. We try to keep our evenings at the bar phone-free, when he's here, to be polite.

The child was crying for his shovel, Anne-Sofie said, he wanted to shovel and sweep the clouds.

JUNE 25, 2016   SATURDAY

Fresno Police shot and killed Dylan Noble after pulling over his pickup truck in response to reports of a man with a rifle. Noble (white, 19) stepped out of his truck with, police say, one arm behind his back. He was shot four times and found not to be carrying a gun.

After a few days the swelling has gone down but my foot still has large zones of black, ankle to mid-sole on both the inside and the outside.

Coffee Yerga Cheffe 1.56 lb @ 10.99	$17.14
Tea Twinings English Breakfast	4.99
Tea Tazo Refresh Mint	5.33
Silver Hills Bread Khorasan	4.32
Natural By Nature Milk Whole Org 1/2 gal	5.49
Yogurt 8 oz 4 @ 1.29	5.16
Yogurt 16 oz	2.20
BioNature Spaghetti Og	1.95
Murray's Ground Chicken	5.16
Snowdance Farm Boneless Breast 0.68 lb @ 9.24	6.28
Ground Beef, McDonald-Grass-Fed 1.01 lb @ 7.15	7.22
Kale – green bunch organic	1.41
Corn 2 @0.49	0.98
Lettuce – romaine organic	1.59
Carrots	1.58
Pluots 0.93 lb @ 3.57	3.32
Peaches – yellow 0.92 lb @ 1.75	1.61
Shallots 0.68 lb @ 1.26	0.86
Tomatoes	5.97
Nature's Path Oatmeal Og Variety	3.28
Avocados – Hass 0.41 lb @ 2.64	1.08
Eggs Pasture – Various	4.62
Scott toilet tissue – white 2 @ 1.08	2.16
	$93.70

JUNE 26, 2016 SUNDAY

When I got to San Francisco, John tells the group, I saw the same rows of low, pastel-colored houses, endless rows, and, past them, the misty cypress trees. The city's changing fast but the suburbs aren't yet, and the offices hadn't. I was there for an onsite, meetings in the same rooms as last time, in the same glassy sun-blasted office parks. The day they broke early, midafternoon, John tells the group, I went down to a place I had heard about but never been, the university's Comparative Zoology Museum.

It was filled with end-of-year school groups: children running, screaming, lying on the floor with their notebooks, making drawings or filling in information for the hunt they were on, now only for treasure or trivia. Behind walls of glass were case after case of previously hunted and gathered animals, not too crowded but definitely massed together: hippo and warthog, moose and elk, deer and dik-dik, down to dozens of squirrels, badgers, dozens of monkeys, all the wolves and foxes, all the rats and other rodents. Separate rooms for the snakes, birds, butterflies, insects, fishes, fossils, frogs, and dinosaur bones. But the rooms filled with children, the cases I couldn't tear myself away from either, held the animals with faces: mostly smiling or grinning, and watching, always watching.

Look into too many of their eyes and you could feel them looking back. Quietly, sadly. All of them expertly—beautifully, if you want to put it that way—stuffed, they live on, lifelike, like life, for students and visitors to look at in turn. Smoke from a pyre, the image rises up: There is a world behind all that glass, the world that used to be ours with the creatures that used to people it. Yes, people. Half of these animals are going to be extinct in our lifetimes, if they're not already, needless to say. It is needless, isn't it?

It's an Old Master painting of the Last Judgment, come to life, or death, Jennifer says, row on row of saints in heaven looking down on the sinners plummeting into Hell and on us. The world of saints and angels in judgment and consolation, the world for which Jan van Eyck and Hans Memling and Jehan Bellegambe could create their great paintings, is still here, still the same. The organic condition. These animals are what the dominions of angels look like now.

Funny you should mention paintings, Jeon said. This was two weeks ago, John?

Thursday before last.

Strange, Jeon said. He'd been having a similar experience just then.

His art teacher had arranged for him to come along on a visit to the studio of Liz Janssen, a painter whose work the teacher thought might help him. Liz would be teaching next fall and the teacher was going to discuss some logistics; she had made an exception and agreed to let the teacher bring Jeon so that he could look around. The teacher kept calling her "Lease," and eventually explained that that was her name, Dutch for

"Lisa," but in Dutch it's spelled "Lies" so she'd changed it professionally.

Her studio was in a cranny of Red Hook, a ways from the last bus stop. When we had walked a few blocks, Jeon told us, we entered the residence of the mysterious Dutchwoman, chosen so that the windows of the roomy floor, which she occupied all of, looked out to the horizon across the bay and the open sky; nothing of the city could be seen but a few buildings and some great clumps of trees. In the other direction, there was mostly unfinished outskirts of the city, construction, board fences, low brick buildings, so the windows showed nothing but those objects resting in a flood of golden light. The magnificent view from the large windows was doubly effective because of an obviously deliberate simplicity and calm in the furnishing of the room itself.

To my surprise, Liz, who gave us a pleasant reception, had nothing Dutch about her, at least in the tall loud blond way one expected. She had black hair and dark eyes, a kind of quiet look I feel like you rarely find anymore, melancholy but not sad if that makes sense. I was also surprised to see no trace of art-making in what I thought was the studio: There were bookshelves, tables with piles of newspapers in various languages, a laptop on the table and a tablet mounted on the wall next to the kitchen area, another near the windows; on the walls, not pictures but maps.

She said she was just making coffee and cleared some space for us to sit down.

Where's the art? I asked her. Is it the maps, or do you do text installations? It's funny, not really, how the last things painters do anymore is paint, no one in school calls themselves a painter unless they work in photography or food art. Like the writers who assemble or edit or film but never write. Liz laughed, said well I guess I'll have to show you my studio after all.

Through a door in the kitchen area that was strangely hard to notice—it seemed small, though you'd think that would make it stand out—was an unbelievably steep and narrow staircase.

Must've brought in a Dutch architect, Iris said. Jeon chuckled and went on.

I had thought from the layout and the steps we'd already climbed that we were on the top floor, but there was another, with low ceilings but frosted skylights. Ranked along the walls were a crowd of life-size figures in glass cases. They were paintings, more beautiful than I'd ever seen outside the popular rooms in museums—they were as good as Richter when he's trying, Vermeer and de Hooch, I remembered again that Liz was Dutch. There were children in a playground, on the slides, around the sprinklers arcing lines of dotted white through the air; there were women, on sofas, in offices; men, too, as people, not officers or statesmen or suitors. None of the paintings had frames, they were all encased in glass, which created a remarkable kind of alternate trompe l'oeil. They were like those museum cases of yours, except the canvases or whatever the paintings were on seemed to float there, so the glass must have been solid but unusually transparent. Maybe there were glass slabs with the painting between them, or painted on one of the strata, not the front one. I think there were subtle 3D effects from painting on different tranches of glass in the same piece, but I didn't have the chance to look closely, the whole mass of the paintings was too overwhelming. And it would have felt like staring at someone on the street, or something.

Then, too, Liz didn't give us much time before fetching from a cabinet a rather large album of paper of the highest quality, thick and almost semi-rigid but soft in texture, not hard and shiny like vellum. There was a lock on the album, and when opened, with a little key from the keychain in Liz's pocket, sheet after sheet gave to view a world of beauty, with no beautiful women, no beautiful landscapes, only men, wavering strangely between realistic and idealized. From their heads they looked like portraits of specific people, Liz's lovers apparently, while their bodies had the exaggerated musculature of drawings by Renaissance masters. It was like a lost Michelangelo or Raphael collection, one man after another, two or three sketches of heads and two or three full-length pictures of each man, except unlike Old Master drawings the men's penises were given the same treatment. Instead of the Old Masters' desultory little soft grubs they were idealized no less than the torsos, the bulging arms and legs that make elderly scholars in these drawings look like bodybuilders. Those dicks were real, some medium-sized and some large, straight or curved, most of them hard, or just recently hard, but not making the drawings pornography any more than the nude chests and big hands did. It was impossible to read either lust or irony into the drawings; these glorifications of male form would seem now simply of a piece with the rest of the drawings, and then again shocking.

Liz turned over the pages, one after another, as unconcernedly as if she were showing us a book on butterflies, only now and then mentioning the name of this man or that: Oh, yes, that's Thomas, that's Amir, that was in London, ah Venice!

We looked on, amazed and speechless, while she turned the leaves bearing so much beauty and talent.

My teacher said she couldn't understand how Liz didn't show these drawings, some of the most remarkable by a living artist she had ever seen, so important in art history, the female gaze . . . Liz smiled. Oh these are just for me.

Now tell me about your work, Liz said to me.

I said my usual thing about abstraction, paint as paint, activating the viewer's emotions without pretending that the object of the painting contained the reality of those emotions or anything else realistically. You've all heard me go on about that, Jeon said. I showed her some images from my portfolio. Well, Liz was having none of it.

The fabrication of a fictitious, artificial, allegorical universe by means of one's own invention and imagination, leaving Nature out of it, is really nothing but fear of hard work. Mere laziness compared to the activity that is simply the indispensable growth of things according to their fixed laws. All creation proceeding from necessity is life and toil; even a simple rose has to help with all its energy, from morning till evening, with its whole physical nature. In the end it fades, but the compensation is that at least it has been a real rose! It's not just wrong to create a world, it's petty, we have to honor this one. The poetry of facts always beats the emotions of artifice.

Then she stopped and chuckled at herself. I'm not preaching at you, she said, but at everyone else. I like your things, actually. Probably because of the contrast to mine.

JUNE 27, 2016   MONDAY

I bought some new jackets for the San Francisco trip, I was telling the group yesterday, my old ones no longer fit, and it was true, at the store I was 44, not 40R anymore. Which I mention because I had a dream that night, after the zoology museum. About dying. I've tried that out for size too now.

It came at the end of a long dream about other things, though death made an appearance there too, when I was getting measured with calipers to be shaved: "44, 44," then, by the neck, "40? that's very bad." Later I'm roaming around a big hotel with a much older woman, blonde, and we can no longer eat . . . then no one can hear us . . . then no one can see us. The motion-sensitive lights in the hall don't come on anymore when we walk past. I realize this means we are dying. We get back to our suite and she goes to bed in the main room, I'm in the back room. But I want very much to have sex with her all of a sudden, so I go out to her bed. There's another bed on the other side of the room with someone in it—an Isaac Bashevis Singer type, and I plan to argue if needed that it's okay, he's used to seeing people have sex next to him, from the camps, he's written about it often. Also, that no one can see us or hear us anymore. But I don't need to argue, I get into bed with her, she says "No, no" but wants to be seduced and soon I'm inside her. Then I see a big black hornet (is it?) with a bulbous body flutter up from the floor past her head—we're now sideways on the bed—and past my hand. I know that it's Death. We keep going, I look down and watch my cock moving in and out of her, then I feel the hornet on my hand. I am sitting across the room then and brushing off, or pulling out, all the little stingers like black dry pine needles from my left hand—the woman is across the room doing something maybe similar, but I don't pay much attention, we are separate now—then they show up: four men in black track suits with black hair and pale, bright white faces. In the dream I think of them as Chinese; they are very polite and friendly, like Vietnamese?, I think. Two are holding, by a wooden bar across the top, a picture painted on some kind of thin stiff felt, of a dark night with a bright white full moon, and they tell me to look into the light. I do, it's nice, then I tear my eyes away and ask them why. They say in a kind voice, "You have died now." They stand in a square and we are supposed to head off at a quick brisk jog with me staying in the middle of their perfect square. I look back at the woman and ask if she can go in my square too—there are men in black with her now too, across the room—and they say in a kind voice, "No, you are alone now." Then I woke up.

My whole foot is bluish now. But it doesn't hurt to walk, as long as I put my weight on my heel, not my toes. I don't even need the crutches anymore when I go to the other rooms. Maybe I should go back to the doctor, but I feel as though it will turn out all right.

JUNE 28, 2016   TUESDAY

Coordinated shootings and suicide bombings at Atatürk Airport in Istanbul today kill 45, wound more than 230, three weeks after what was previously known as the June 2016 Istanbul bombing (12, 51).

I watched a talk online today over lunch, given by a man dressed all in black except for his sandals over gray socks. No matter how many times I see them, I always think the wireless mics they use are an orange tumor on the speaker's face, even after I remember what they are. Why did they make them look like that.

The talk was about a painter who fled Russia to the West, from the Revolution; found himself in France, where in genteel poverty he discovered a true talent for abstract painting—childhood memories of snowy steppes and samovars obliterated, some would say transformed but I'm not so sure, the speaker said. He reduced, reduced, reduced the human form to a stripe, the landscape to blocks and squares. For all their cubism and modernism, the French do not seem to have been able to go so far. Picasso was Spanish.

But to return to our Russian aristocrat fallen on hard times, he was still in Paris when the Nazis came, painting for days and nights on end in his studio and refusing to pay attention to events around him. His family starved, his young child died, I cannot understand how he didn't go mad too—in the whole crazy story of his life, this is what I am least able to understand, how anyone can lose a child and live, he said. It used to happen all the time, of course, and still does, I think of the soccer-friend who missed a month or two of games and then we heard that he and his parents had lost sight of his eighteen-month-old in the mall for a minute during which the son and grandson had fallen into a fountain with six inches of water in it and drowned, he was back at our weekly pick-up games, I couldn't talk to him even look at him I never played soccer with that group again. Our Russian painter carried on, the speaker said, work from '46, '47 started to appear, a gray dismal palette for a while and then back to his usual look. Maybe it was from then on that his grays became so beautiful, he painted the most beautiful grays since Fra Angelico if you ask me, he said. There were the years of furious output—'49, '50, '52—and before too much longer he had jumped out a window overlooking the Mediterranean at last. So much for our Russian painter.

Someone in the question and answer session made a long rambling more-of-a-comment, and in the middle of the speaker's answer he said: All the world's religions and philosophies enjoin mankind to worship its memories.—

JUNE 29, 2016　　WEDNESDAY

My foot is neither better nor worse. I spend most of my days in the apartment, but still hobble out sometimes.

Midday at the café around the corner, back from the West Coast.

Is someone sitting here?

Decaf soy latte!
Here. Thanks
It's hot
Ooh!
This is decaf? Sorry, just to check, I ordered a decaf, right?
Right, decaf.

Okay thanks

I don't like it here, it's too masculine. And you have to bow down and kiss the barista's feet, I hate that, it's not like it's wine, it's coffee. I just want a decent cup of coffee. I don't want to have to act impressed about the Ethiopian's fruit notes to some hipster micro-
Hahaha
micromanaging a drip filter.

I hear you're not sleeping with her.
. . . Our relationship hasn't, uh, whatever . . .
No, I'm impressed. She's keeping you interested. I like that.

Do you mind if I sit here?
Sure.
Thanks
. . .
Is that
Sure thing, man. I'm just hanging out waiting for the drink.

What? Yeah . . .
Thanks, oh thanks . . .
What? . . .
You're breaking up . . .

Were you on line?

I was just getting into line. But you go first, I'm not in any hurry.

Thanks

Did you call out a small single latte?

No. You're next, sorry

Sorry, no problem. It's crazy in here.

Yeah

Is it always like this?

Well, yeah. Every Saturday and Sunday. Weekends too.

Some Overheard Haiku

Yeah, the internet's
fucked up, I don't know, I, I
texted Renée and . . .

"She has a home phone.
Who has home phones?" "Yeah different
lifestyle." "Totally."

Everyone has to
move out the last of the month
but the point *is,* that . . .

"No! You can't *do* that!"
"(That's why we're not having kids.)"
"I'm, I'm gonna, I'm . . ."

"Hey, man, are there tendons and ligaments in the bottom of your foot?"

("Yes.")

I met this Jewish guy and he told me right away how much money he makes

I've only kissed, I've only ever hooked up with one Jewish guy. Some girls are obsessed.

I know. I'm never going to date another Jewish guy.
I wish there was a dating thing for *this* neighborhood.
You can never really tell what the guy's all about.
I'm also just *so* picky.

Is this free?

> The thing is that I
> don't feel very much respect
> for myself right now
>
> I, I empathize
> with this, she doesn't aggress
> down, she aggresses up.

What kind of donuts are these?

They're vegan, we've got blueberry, glazed, with Oreos on . . .

Uh it's okay
top . . .
I like milk, sorry.
What?
In my donuts, I mean
Oh. Vegan's a problem
Just in donuts . . .
I understand.

Anyone sitting here?

It's not a book proposal, is it? I hate that shit. *Times* magazine, *Esquire*, *Atlantic*'s the worst, you think you're reading an article and it's a pitch for a book deal: My Year Eating Vegetables! My Year Keeping Talmudic Law . . . And I'm Not Even Jewish! Fifteen Marriage Therapies When My Husband And I Are Pretty Happy Anyway! And you know that if you do ever read the book it'll feel like a padded-out book pitch. It's all just one big bullshit gimmick, plus it's always trying too hard, because it just wants to sell itself.

No, no book pitch . . .

Thank fucking god.

Yeah, trying too hard, I know. I was writing this email the other day and I realized I was trying to try hard and also to not try too hard and at the same time trying to try not to look like I was trying not to try too hard

She says she's not a vegetarian but basically she is.
Yeah, I don't like to say I'm vegetarian either. People start to get
Veggie Danish!
Danish
For here right?
Yeah

Did you know the number one import in America is coffee?
Really? That makes sense. America is a big land of coffee drinkers. Rakesh, you drink coffee every day? And you drink coffee every day? I have coffee every day? Think how much coffee that makes

Vadim? Vadim?

This seat free?

Yeah, he's not in your status bracket

Which do you recommend, the lemon bread or a scone. Which is moister.
Cappuccino!! Moister? Um,
The lemon bread?
Yeah, hey, which is *moister*, lemon bread or scone.

Oh the lemon bread, definitely.

Okay, good. I'll take a lemon bread and a small single espresso

The author, who has made every effort to create a gripping narrative, feels that he should pause here for reflection.

Someday they will say of us that we were living in a strange time, the kind that usually follows revolutions or the decline of great empires. It was no longer the heroic fervor of midcentury upheavals, the glamorous vices of concentrations of power, or the skeptical soullessness and insane orgies of the latest bubbles. It was an age in which despair and material comfort, technological wizardry and political malaise, and a paradoxical freedom, both from criticism and to endlessly criticize, were mixed together, along with deep but narrow enthusiasms, the renunciation of utopias, condescension toward the past, weariness of the present, and pessimism for the future. Material man no longer knew how badly it yearned for violets and crimson roses from Athena or Isis. Our nightly dreams, where this goddess made us feel the shame of having turned away from her eternal youth, were forgotten each morning.

At our best, we renounced ambition, unable to imagine a goal worth striving for and repelled by the constant anxious and greedy striving all around us from which we retreated to ivory towers or solitary gardens. Led by our memories, and nostalgias for what we could no longer remember, we drank blindness to our surroundings from the silver cup of legend, intoxicating ourselves with literature, music, and love. Love, however, of vague forms, the only forms left now that the sexual and psychological mysteries of past eras had been brought into the harsh white light of clarity. So we preferred imagined, unapproachable souls to the bodies all too visible and available around us. We turned away from princes and slaves, charisma and coquetry, everything that past generations and centuries had told us we should want, and we had no vocabulary to describe how their absence felt, or what it might mean.

It was a time, they will say, when we had lost the thread of the story. The end we felt nigh was no Apocalypse, no Antichrist—it was the end of we knew not what, and so there was no putting our spiritual house in order, no reflections on the journey traveled, no whole life flashing before our eyes. No whole life. Even the earth-shaking events of that time never felt *grand*. We went about our dying business.

The greatest book of that time, they may say, if anyone still says such things, was a collection of photographs: pictures of oilfields, tankers, refineries, cars, roads, factories, salvage, polluted water, skies on fire. Large-format shots, most of them from slightly overhead so that the picture plane tipped us in. For compositions so impersonal—almost none had any people—they felt deeply personal; our world, our places. Turning page after oversized page of this book made you feel it, know it: Your place in the world and what we have made the world become.

Someone sitting here?

Hey guys, *okay, gimme a call,* thanks for coming over

JUNE 30, 2016   THURSDAY

Shambolic Boris Johnson, who apparently didn't really mean it about that whole Brexit thing, has withdrawn from the race for prime minister.

We've hit analog retro, Jeon said. I saw a guy on the train—expensive sneakers with no socks, beard, shaved head, Freitag bag—with a picture of a wall of LPs on his black t-shirt. His iPhone case looked like a cassette tape. Side A. The phone was a little too big to be a real cassette but the label was designed well, close enough to the real thing to fool me. He put his audiophile buds in his ears, cords running back over each ear, and twiddled away with his thumb for the next twenty minutes.

Someone else I saw today, even more stylish shoes, had an expensive pale suede shoulder bag with a honking big tape reel (SONY) attached to the side—not a picture of a reel: actual metal disks, like some kind of fender to keep dings off the suede?

I remember last spring, Anne-Sofie said, or was it the spring before? when Starbucks was selling a CD called *My Last Mix Tape*? Nostalgia for the old plus a lesson for the young. "In the distant ancient '90s," it said on the back, "The Mix Tape was an essential form of communication—a way of saying 'Here's how I feel' . . ."

Actually, Chris said, that's just how they market to the olds. They pretend to be talking to young people because no one wants to think that nostalgia is the only reason to like what they like.

But '90s music isn't just nostalgic for us, it's cool for the twenty-year-olds!

What twenty-year-old buys CDs?

JULY 1, 2016   FRIDAY

Warmer to much-warmer-than-average conditions dominated across much of the globe's surface, resulting in the highest temperature departure for June since global temperature records began in 1880. This was also the 14th consecutive month the monthly global temperature record has been broken.

Five of six continents had at least a top five warm June, with North America observing a record high average temperature for June; no land areas had a record cold temperature during June 2016. Averaged as a whole, the global temperature across land surfaces for June 2016 was 2.23° F above the 20th century average—the 34th consecutive June with temperatures above average.

The last time global land surface temperatures were below average in June was in 1982 (by 0.09° F).

The worldwide ocean surface temperature was 1.39° F above the 20th century average, the highest global ocean temperature for June in the 137-year record; the 10th highest departure from average among all 1,638 months in the record; and the 40th consecutive June with above-average global ocean temperatures.

The 12 highest monthly global ocean temperature departures from the average have all occurred in the past 12 months.

I have not seen anything written, really written, about those months in the summer of 2009 as hundreds of thousands of gallons of oil a day, day after day after day after day, poured into the Gulf of Mexico from an exploded well deep underwater. I think it is the defining moment (extended moment) of our age, reshaping us more than the Kennedy assassination, moon landing, Tiananmen, fall of the Wall, 9/11. The articles written on it have been long, and they put the events into perspective, the comfort of narrative perspective: deregulation, Republican hatred of government responsibility, criminal corporate negligence; heroic individual efforts, technical constraints overcome, a Hollywood race against time. While it was happening, though, we all went about our business—a business requiring massive consumption of petroleum, from gas for our cars to plastic bags to shipping for everything in the world we buy. All the while being forced to think about and know what was happening in the Gulf of Mexico, and know that nothing could be done about it. I remember a picnic that June. Good food, children playing, warm sun, and the scientist from the South not wanting to bum us out or anything, he said, but telling us about the oil's effects on the plant life on the coast, how that extra bonus piece of destruction we hadn't even considered would take out enough trees to increase worldwide global warming by another however many percent. Those magazine writers could have saved themselves the trouble, because the narrative of the BP spill was quite simple and we all knew it, all felt it: There Is Nothing To Be Done. We can't just stop drilling and mining and exploiting, even if we somehow ran the world—and if it wasn't a deepwater well in the Gulf of Mexico, it would be something else next time. (Six months later came Fukushima.) It wasn't a single incident you could second-guess or explain away or have some other cathartic experience about, it was month after month of helplessness—the government could do nothing, the oil company itself was trying as hard as it could by that point, even it was clearly on our side for once, and it could do nothing. Something Obama had said earlier, during the election, was reported that summer: He had been asked by a journalist what was something personal he'd done to go green and he had given the right kind of answer but then vented in private later: "What I'm thinking in my head is, 'Well, the truth is, Brian, we can't solve global warming because I fucking changed the light bulbs I use in my house. It'll be because of something collective.'" He didn't yet know how constrained collective action would be too, but he was right about the first part: Individual action doesn't make a difference. That summer of the spill, it was starting to sink in.

It was the spring everyone had Labrunie handbags. Not everyone, not like Birkin knockoffs or Burberry—middlebrow and sinking fast—but you saw them around the city if you looked. I looked. I had touched one once or twice, enough to keep a sense memory of the hard tingle the ridges made if you ran your palm across the surface one way, the smooth slide of moving it the other way, so I felt something in my hand whenever I saw the iridescent blue, rippling visually like the tide flinging down its wrinkled little waves. In the New York light, or against the colors its bearers preferred, or for whatever reason, the bag usually looked silver-blue like the water (not the sky) on an overcast beach, but the shimmers could be sapphire or sky blue, turquoise, bruise-black, even so rich it shaded into emerald. It was like some kind of mood ring, even though it never seemed to match the mood of the woman carrying it, as far as I could tell; maybe it matched the mood of the world, the weather. Maybe it matched mine. Maybe that was Labrunie's secret.

JULY 2, 2016   SATURDAY

The day I wrote that, I hurt my foot again, my other foot. Turning around, limping on a heel, I swung around and smashed the second-to-smallest toe of the other foot against a little stepstool I was using in the kitchen. It was right up against the cupboards so there was no give, and instead of stubbing my toe I seem to have broken it. By the next day there was a strip of black on that foot too, diagonally down to the base and halfway around the side—bend sinister—with red and white too, I could describe it all in more detail but why? I didn't see a doctor either, I would have had to describe it to them.

It was hard to walk on that foot but more than anything it was confusing: trying to protect my hurt foot by putting my weight, say, on the other foot, but that was the one with the real injury in need of consideration. It seemed symbolical of something. The one with real damage suffering out of some misguided effort to coddle the other.

Other than that, and the strange premonition in yesterday's writing, is it not worth mentioning? Though is the first foot's injury, for that matter? What is?

Dream about the Dark Angel de Vitesse, which in the dream meant "youth" although it actually means "speed" in French. The Demon Velocity. It stayed with me—not the dream, I completely forgot what happened, but the angel, behind my left shoulder, pushing me onward. Painted by an Italian artist, fifteenth century; gray, almost black; long fangs or tusks. Nothing banishes him except patience. Anything you can do by waiting is natural and good, anything that requires haste is artificial and dangerous, to yourself and to the world.

SIBERIAN CHILD DIES AFTER CLIMATE CHANGE THAWS ANTHRAX-INFECTED REINDEER. 1,500 reindeer die in a single day. Researchers have found pieces of the 1918 Spanish flu virus in corpses buried in mass graves in Alaska's tundra; there's also likely smallpox and the bubonic plague buried in Siberia.

Iris said she didn't want to go over to her boyfriend's house because she'd probably stain the sheets, at this time of the month, and Jennifer said: He'd mind that? What the hell is that guy's problem? How can he not understand about sheets?

What about sheets? Iris said.

You know how when Viking warriors died bravely in battle they went to Valhalla? Getting killed didn't mean they lost, it meant they had lived and died in the most glorious and honorable way you possibly can, and as a reward they were taken to heaven. When sheets get stained from sex they go to Sheet Valhalla. It's their eternal reward for fulfilling their destiny. Throwing away stained sheets is an incredible privilege, it's one of the most beautiful and perfect things we can do. Nothing better can happen to a sheet. We should be happy for them.

Plato called Heroes those who can also be called *foreign and pilgrim Daemons,* but not the aqueous Daemons who are Daemons by their nature, Josh quoted.

JULY 3, 2016   SUNDAY

Bright white glare low in the sky, the grass tinged yellow: summer rainstorm.

At least 346 people were killed today, more than 246 injured, in a series of coordinated bomb attacks in Baghdad, including a car bomb exploding in the middle of a busy market.

Yesterday, the early morning of long weekend, Trump tweeted out a Jewish star on a big pile of money. Today reports emerge that it had been lifted from an outright racist site, known for photoshopping Hillary Clinton's portrait into a swastika, etc. Trump insists it was "just a basic star." Elie Wiesel has died, and Trump has not commented, and if you read Trump's books, a lawyer tweetstorms, it's clear he counterproductively micromanages so having another hundred staffers on the campaign isn't going to fix anything. Trump is already overwhelmed as part-time manager (he spends time on his other businesses) with thirty staffers. And this means there's no bandwidth for routine regrets on death of Wiesel. Of course, where that lands Trump and nation if he accidentally wins is scary. Post-January planning hasn't begun, and Trump seems to plan to wing it with thousands of appointments in a two-month sprint while he's learning on the job.

Last month, in San Francisco, after the offsite was over, I saw on my phone that the Empire was closing at the end of the month—a movie theater I'd loved when I lived in the Bay Area. I decided to see whatever they were showing that night, for the memories.

It was Jim Jarmusch, *Dead Man*, with Johnny Depp, which I'd seen in the '90s when it came out, but which hadn't made an impression on me. Well, it must have been a movie from the future, which meant from now. Now I thought *Dead Man*, let me come right out and say it, was the greatest movie I'd ever seen about America. *Apocalypse Now*, *Citizen Kane*, *The Philadelphia Story*, you name it.

Music in the darkness. An accountant in a Lewis Carroll checked suit, leaving behind the wreck of a personal life and Cleveland, heads out West, where he finds gun nuts, autocrat plutocrats, Indian genociders, and what's left of folkways and wilderness. He finds the world of Machine—the town he reaches at the end of the line is called Machine, a world of sex and death—but in flight from Machine there is beauty, mystery, friendship, history, a new self that is also old, and poetry. What we see is crisp and liquid at once in its black and white; what we hear behind the story is primal music, melody drenched in electricity; the movement of things is slow; there are fades to white between the scenes, like semicolons of time.

The Indian who befriends this accountant is named Nobody, a nod to Homer;—his Indian name translates as He Who Talks Loud Saying Nothing, a James Brown joke at Ridiculous Indian Name Hollywood's expense. There was a group of about eight Indians in the audience at the Empire, one of them older than the others, maybe a Native American Studies class with teacher or just circle of friends, and they laughed at several of the lines in Cree that Jarmusch left unsubtitled, murmured at the Pacific coast Indian village at the end, cheered and whooped over the credits. This was a film for not only my America.

Afterward I went looking around on the internet for more. There was a master's thesis in anthropology on the six Makah actors and two Makah set artists who had made the recreated Northwest Coast village so authentic. A think piece on the soundtrack. I liked an essay that called *Dead Man* obviously some kind of Western, but more like the ghostly burnt-out shell of a Western, commandeered for sullen and obscure purposes.

One article explained allegory, which I'd never really understood: when something means something else, a story that isn't the real story but points at one. If a man named Christian is on a difficult road and meets people named Hypocrisy, Laziness, and False Faith, who try to keep him from reaching the Heavenly City, then this isn't a story about a real man on a real road. You get a lot of that kind of story in church, or in school. There's another kind of allegory, though, where everything that happens is really inside a single person. When Peace comes with a flaming sword and slices Violence to bits, Peace is not a peaceful person, the way Christian is Christian; it's a state of the soul which needs to defeat its enemies, Rage and Wrath, by any means necessary.

Once you personify Peace, though, you give it something more than an abstract nature, this article pointed out, so that the second kind of allegory is always a bit of the first too. Which creates a tension: How can Peace lay waste with a flaming sword? When Chastity kills Lust, the monastic ascetic isn't killing a hot babe, just ignoring her—but telling the story this way brings some violence into it. It makes you wonder: Is the rejection of desire a kind of violence? It gets harder to tell the difference between what's on the outside and what's on the inside.

In *Dead Man*, Thelma Russell, known as Thel, is the woman Depp's character sleeps with, or is about to sleep with, before her angry lover, the son of the boss, barges in and shoots. She dives to protect him; the bullet passes through her, kills her, and lodges in him, and from that point on he is a dead man. "Thel" in Greek is Θελ, Will or Desire—Θέλω is to want. So dying begins with the death of desire, of the striving will. The Boss's son loved Drive or Will, naturally—his family rules Machine, he wants power, mastery, ownership. But she does not love him back, or at least she betrays him: It is impossible to keep Desire all to yourself, corner the market on striving, use up all that resource. The Will gives herself to receptive outsiders.

It's the most forced interpretation in the world, based on sheer coincidence between Θελ and Thel. But it isn't. Depp's character bears the name William Blake, and his Indian friend thinks he *is* William Blake, the poet, in the flesh or reborn, and Blake's first engraved poem is called "Thel," about a woman who dies before experiencing love.

Is this enough? the article asks. Can we really believe this is what Jarmusch meant? I don't know. But one way to describe Depp's incredible screen presence in this movie, the article says and that Friday night in the cold light of the laptop screen I agreed, is that like no other actor since Buster Keaton, sitting gloomily on the wheel-rod of a train or in a hundred other moments, he embodies passivity. He shows through his acting the act of not acting, what comes after the death of the will.

So *Dead Man* tempts us to decode it—track Blake's other poems through the movie, for instance. (The whole plot is about tracking William Blake.) But Jim Jarmusch's mind doesn't work like that, not consistently;—he isn't writing a master's thesis, on Blake or Indians or The West or Death, though his masterly movie says more about those things than anything I know. The allegory in the movie is a kind of detour, which is what people complain about: Why have a young man named Christian reject Mr. Badman and walk through the Valley of Despond instead of just saying what you mean? *Dead Man* has the parallels without making too rigid an equation. It's the gap, the displacement. It means something that Depp is named William Blake, but nothing too obvious, too logical. William Blake is not just Wm. Blake—who among us is? even he wasn't— so you can't just forget the accountant and look at the poet. What then do you do? How to say that Blake *is* Blake, that Machine *is* America, that dying *is* dying?

I click around more, I think more about the forest they wander through—beautiful in the film's black and white, filled with monsters and lovers and wonders. I search for DEAD MAN DEPP FOREST: only academic articles come up. The forest is formlessness; a "wandering wood" is not a wood that roams around but the wood of our wandering, the wood of going astray. If beasts are dangers within oneself, the forest they inhabit can only be the self. Thus the body is at once the castle or machine of the soul and the forest of beasts around it.

I couldn't read that stuff for long and followed a random link from <u>forest</u> to a short story somewhere else. I was in a birch woods, Breughel country in winter, it said. The long house with the mossy roof and window after window in two rows was set far back from the road, separating the woods from a large square meadow sloping down into the countryside; my rooms were on the meadow side, across from my parents', and looked out onto a few minutes a day of yellow sunlight, glowing off of the ice crusts on the grass, and a few other hours, not many, of gray daylight or falling snow. Silent black birds with long straight tails flew by, on their sides, showing profiles as if from above.

The winter woods were bare but interesting. If I headed away from the driveway, past the pile of felled logs too big for firewood, I could get lost myself down in the ravine or up where a fence on the hillside forced me to turn back and get disoriented. I sometimes balanced on the tree stumps that held the fence posts, swung a winter-coated leg over the timid old barbed wire, and jumped heavily down on the other side, sinking in snowy mud to my boot tops. I could walk across other people's fields and once made it to the paved roads of the next village. Or, getting through a widely spaced wood fence, it would be harder to push through the thick-grown thorn hedge, hunched over, leaving lichen-green smears on my coat, but that was on the meadow side, with the two horses, the mice who looked brown and natural—health food for falcons—and a gentle donkey with an enormous, slow-to-move head, like a papier-mâché actor's mask of a donkey; it was so big it must be hollow inside. His fur when I reached up to touch it was surprisingly rough and harsh, and crusted with mud. The woods at that time of year had lichen on the north sides of the trunks and dry empty seed pods and once, just once, threads of gossamer in the sunlight.

Otherwise the woods were almost uninhabited, except for Reuben: a neighbor's boy who roamed and tromped and showed me his favorite places, the special trees or clearings. He liked to guide. His father had died last year, unexpectedly, his mother worked and he was often alone. Before long he trusted me enough to show me his camp, a sort of lean-to he had built all by himself, collecting bare branches for the walls and thick branches of pine needles to prop up and layer over each other as a roof. He had a long thin saw to trim branches or cut down dead saplings with. He had put the whole structure together without nails or tape, just rope and leaning; inside (well, the walls weren't done, so there wasn't exactly an "inside"—say "underneath") were a low plain bench and some pots and pans for an imaginary, self-reliant kitchen. I was impressed and trailed around after him for a long time, as Reuben showed me his quarries and sources for the best pine branches and saplings.

The other life in the woods was a box of bees at the far corner, by the bend in the main road. Just a crate at this time of year, nothing even worth walking over to look at. But from this distance you could hear the hum of the summer swarm, the air on a hillside filled with sound. A whole world poured out from that cold, dead crate—dead on the outside—like a genie from a bottle. This was the summer you have not experienced yet, a summer to come, on a gentle meadow, or September, the month of yellow, sunflowers and asters and falling elm leaves, and the sound of that yellow is the buzz of the bees.

Summer is somewhere inside you, invisible, its golden combs dripping with honey-colored sunlight.

At your center, your centermost center, sits the Queen. Out from her emanates the world.

The bee with its jaunty stripes and delicate wings has gone out into the field so that you can hoard it in you through your winter.

The hum of the bees is the sound of the world, the way the rush of the wind is like the roar of the sea.

"Buried animals, as we know by experience," I read, (I mean the narrator of the online story said he read,) "transform themselves into flowers and thence into bees, who enjoy the countryside and eagerly work on their treasure, their dearest hope." Bright daisy, soft hum, acanthus, orchid petaled in sex and sting. The black blot of smiling yellow pansies—are they flowers or their friends?

The story made me remember summer bees from the park, as a child, on the grassy hills outside the playground, beyond the fence. More than once, they crawled on my nose, my lips. Everything stopped; I didn't try to shoo or shake the bee off, and maybe get stung; I already knew that a prick on the finger could make my whole arm swell, could make me stop breathing and fall to the ground. I didn't know what a sting on the face might do. But we understood each other, the bee and I—the rules were clear to us both. I wonder why William Blake in *Dead Man*, on the opening train journey, reads *The Illustrated Bee Journal*, advertising hives and queens and psychic healers. It has a railroad timetable on the back cover, but still.

It's hard to keep a bee in your sight against trees or hills, you have to lie low to fetch him against the sky. Blue and white, complementary colors to yellow and black: a secret logic. You have to be in an open space, not in the woods. After circling a while to get its bearings it will fly off—make a bee-line—and come back twenty minutes or an hour later; if you've dabbed its back with paint powder you will know it's the same one. You can sight along the bee-line, take other readings from farther along or from other points of the compass and triangulate to find the hive, if honey or hives are what you're after.

All of this lay forgotten and dormant within me for decades, until the black and white forest Johnny Depp passes through so deeply the second time I saw *Dead Man*.

Please forgive these digressions.—

As I hunted for more essays, more background and takes on the movie, the browser autofill started changing. At the beginning of the night I could look up DEAD MAN NEIL YOU and it would fill in: ng soundtrack. DEAD MAN JARmusch depp. ALLEGORY DEAD MAN movie. As the night wore on, new suggestions started appearing: DEAD

MAny how many. DEADly shooting. DEAth toll orlando. That's how I heard.

"What does it smell like?" Thel asks William Blake, holding out to him one of her paper roses. "Paper," he says. "Well it is paper," she says.

JULY 4, 2016   MONDAY

It's a different kind of memory: Just the shape of it, mother and two daughters, no details or texture. My life as an abstract painting.

JULY 5, 2016   TUESDAY

In Baton Rouge, Louisiana, Alton Sterling, a 37-year-old black man known around the neighborhood as CD Man, was shot six times at close range while being held down on the ground, killed, by two Baton Rouge Police Department officers. They were responding to a report that a man in a red shirt was selling CDs, and that he had used a gun to threaten a man outside a convenience store.

Low call of a tenor sax, practicing in the park. Image. I've seen him before but only hear him now, behind a tree, a few runs and snatches of melody—"Dream of You," "Dizzy's Business," "I Heard It Through the Grapevine." It's the long pauses between the arcs and the lines—he is practicing, not playing—that make his music into an image. Each melody, each squeak and cry, is separated from the others by a break in the empty space. The image has time to breathe in the empty air.

Ben is telling us about a documentary he saw, on yak herders. Every year the tribe takes their herd to the year's grazing grounds, or four of them do, there are always four men on the journey. Each plays one of the four roles—the roles are more important than each year's individual participants. It is a very structural understanding of group endeavors, I like that, Ben says. Every journey, this practice tells us, has a mother, a father, an animal master, and a younger son or novice with almost no responsibilities. These are four men of roughly the same age. Someone to tend to the cooking and housekeeping; someone in charge of navigation and defense; someone in charge of the herd. The Youngest Son is the fascinating role: Why make sure, why have it be necessary, to travel with someone inherently or structurally inadequate and foolish? Is it to have a scapegoat, for the others to blame or vent frustrations on? If so, that job, which seems easiest, must be the hardest—spiritual lightning rod, psychic cesspit, therapy dog. But he seems to be loved, not blamed. Is it so there's always someone for the others to help? A group of pure equals can't get along in the long run, that feels right to me, and wise. Not all of us are cut out to be a youngest son, only to have one.

Dinner parties are the same, Ben goes on. There always has to be a mother, a boss, a wild man, and a listener.

We're not as wise a culture, Anne-Sofie says.

If the wild man doesn't get wasted but just tells stories of bad dates or getting fired, he slides into the other form of the type, the charity case. But the last few parties I've been to haven't had that, they've been too dominated by the mother or the boss. They've been like work, or homework.

Maybe that's why nobody has dinner parties anymore, Chris says. Who has dinner parties?

We're not as wise a culture, Anne-Sofie says.

JULY 6, 2016   WEDNESDAY

Philando Castile, a gentle and soft-spoken man who served food in local elementary schools in Saint Paul, Minnesota, but black, so he might as well have been Genghis Khan shrieking war cries from the steppes, was shot and killed in Falcon Heights by police during a routine traffic stop for a broken tail light—seven bullets pumped into the car, in front of his girlfriend and her two-year-old daughter. His one tattoo was of the Twin Cities he so loved. The cop will say that he, the cop, was afraid, and Castile being black is sufficient reason for that, and fear is sufficient reason for a policeman to shoot seven bullets, so there seems to be a certain structural problem standing in the way of conviction and accountability here.

Roger Ailes, the chairman of Fox News and the most powerful man in American media, was accused of forcing out prominent female anchor Gretchen Carlson after she refused his sexual advances and complained to him about his persistent harassment. Carlson, a longtime Fox employee who left the network last month, described Ailes in her lawsuit as a loutish and serial sexual harasser. The *New York Times* finds the accusation startling, for Mr. Ailes typically enjoys absolute loyalty from his employees, says the *New York Times*. There seem to be certain structural problems standing in the way of accountability here.

Trump re-raised an issue most thought better left dropped, saying the only thing he was sorry for was that someone in his campaign had taken the original six-pointed-star image down. And after being interrupted during his press conference by a pesky mosquito that he couldn't seem to swat away, he said "I don't like mosquitoes," twice. "Speaking of mosquitoes, hello Hillary. How are you doing?" The crowd erupted in laughter.

I know one person who actually looks like a demon, I mean physically, Keith tells us. Like a Tibetan tantric demon. You don't need a red or green face, skull necklace, seven heads, flaming vajra wand; even bulging eyes matter less, in turns out, than a squarish face and tightly curled hair and an emanation of evil and destruction. I'd heard stories of Avi's depthless evil toward people I didn't know very well, Keith said, but he was nice enough to me and to my friends. Still, he did seem capable of doing anything, truly anything. He just hadn't chosen to around me, not yet.

A white woman on the street—young, punk pink hair, big boots, walking with a limp; seeing my limp probably the only reason why she smiled at me. Ripped black punk tank top with letters scrawled in all-caps white: DROP / F**KING / DEAD.

JULY 7, 2016   THURSDAY

In Dallas, Texas, at a protest against the police killings of Alton Sterling and Philando Castile, an Army Reserve Afghan War veteran named Micah Xavier Johnson opened fire on a group of police officers, killing five and injuring nine as well as two civilians. He was reportedly angry over police shootings of black men and stated that he wanted to kill white people, especially white police officers.

Comparisons to 1968 start appearing in the media, the tearing of the American social fabric. Sober responses—recalling RFK, MLK, tens of thousands dead in Vietnam, riots in hundreds of cities, police clubbing and killing protestors instead of protecting them, this isn't the same—don't seem to help. There is something in the analogy that seems to hold.

The group in the narrow courtyard behind the bar starts talking about the late sixties, the seventies. Scott tells us his mother was really sick one summer, her arms almost paralyzed, and his father was taking care of her until English cousins came to take charge. He, Scott, was brought back home.

It was the summer of 1979. Skylab. He was at summer camp, but it was a grownup's theater camp upstate, so the menu board had Skylab notices every day—eighteen days to go, sixteen, fourteen; over the Indian Ocean, Europe, the Midwest, the South Pacific. Is it possible? Scott says now. Was it really all just a big joke?

We didn't know how innocent we were. We never seem to stop having to say that.

The aunt showed up with armloads of hydrangeas; the other aunt had flown straight from her UN job in Nepal, where she collected carpets. For days we were full of tiger-skin rugs and hydrangeas. There were two cousins, playmate children to replace the ones from camp. It was a very happy summer, despite my mother's illness.

Once, that summer, walking west on the south side of a street, in the shadow of a block-long building, he'd had a vision: the sun slanted in up ahead, from the crossstreet, and there, in the sun, where what must have been young leaves or seed pods caught in the wind, darting and circling like giant daytime fireflies or, simply, fairies of light. They didn't fall through the sunbeams—they flitted in them. By the time I got to the cross street, the phenomenon was gone, like dense fogs, like dreams. The scene almost brought tears to my eyes.

But the strange thing is I forgot it, Scott says. I never once thought of it in all the years and decades since, until it came back to me in a flash a couple months ago when I saw a young woman with long dark hair, in an orange, expensive dress, a folder in her hand from the college around the corner—it is graduation day—and she is crying, silent savage tears from a deep and vulnerable center. What could be making her cry like that? Not a recent, isolated insult; not something expected that she could have prepared for, like the pain of graduating and being thrust out into the world.

Is she beautiful?—Is it a better image if she is or if she isn't?

I have no idea how or why it came back to me then. A woman crying on her graduation day has nothing I can think of to do with a New York street in Skylab summer.

In the rain, the path in the park outside my window was suddenly white, as if miscast from December. It is a wide paved Olmsted road, usually gray, I would have thought, but actually now that I look again it's brown, or yellow with blue-gray shadows in direct sunlight. Nothing is ever what we think it is, is it. Even when something is surprisingly different, what it's different from turns out to be a surprise too. The thin film of rain on the paved path must be acting like a mirror, reflecting an overcast white sky. Image.

JULY 8, 2016   FRIDAY

Keith starts calling himself (((Keith))) online.

I'm moving my books from one office to another, by subway, Josh says, in two big shopping bags. A woman is sitting across from me staring into her red leather Kindle case, legs crossed most unsprawlingly, elbows pinning a white cardigan tight to her sides. The feminine form of not presuming to take up space. She looked down at my heavy, bulging bags and smiled, made eye contact, looked down amused again. We're opposites, I wish she said, raising her e-book slightly, like a wineglass in a toast.

Next to me sat a man in silence, South Chinese, staring at his smartphone: Lucky Wheel, wheels within wheels, spinning silently or rather the sound locked tight in the cord traveling up to his earbuds. The masculine form. Skulls and hearts and pentagrams whirling, as flicks of his thumbs make the pictures of flippers shoot the picture of a pinball up into the constellation. While I turn back to the poem I am reading in a slim paper book, and it says the same thing:

> There is no noise as the stars turn. Lustrous signs, they advertise themselves to themselves.
>
> Powers, intelligences, sensualities

do not emerge from the closets of light.
Literary as this all sounds, I am not making it up, I promise you. You can check, the poem at least (p. 14). I don't know how to check the video game.

All that is merely sensible objects to or yields to the urgencies of ours to dream the world, Josh says.

Later, Pam is talking about plays. A guy took me out once when I was abroad, took me to a play—would that *ever* happen here in New York, to anyone under sixty? And he didn't say it was to help me practice the language or anything, no excuses. Just a date at the theater! There were two characters, He and She, no proper names to prove how real they are, and the set was unbelievably artsy and pretentious, at least that's what I thought at the time, but I still remember it now, so I guess it probably worked. It was a one-act and the stage was bare at first, with spotlights on the two characters, and throughout the play a dozen or so logs were slowly, slowly lowered from the ceiling, vertically. This looming mass of pillars crowding down. He and She had been pacing, dashing, circling around the whole time they were talking, and once the logs got low enough He and She kept moving, ignoring the obstacles—all the movements were carefully choreographed, but they looked as natural as they had before. The logs were attached at the top with a bunch of green ropes stretched diagonally in different directions, and as the whole contraption got lower we could see the ropes, and eventually we got the symbolic forest thing (abstract treetops). It was strangely suspenseful to watch them all coming slowly, slowly down, wondering what would happen when they hit the floor of the stage. I forgot to mention, there was one log, by far the biggest, that came down diagonally—there must have been a thin cord we couldn't see holding the bottom end—and when the trees hit the ground in the middle of one of She's speeches the lower end of the big one did too and the tree reached all the way across the stage, like a giant redwood falling in the forest. The set stayed like that for the last few minutes, giving a lot of extra tension to the dialogue: The trees could just stop moving? Just like that? What would happen next? At the climax, which we didn't realize was the climax until this happened, the green ropes on the top of the slanting tree were released all at once and it came crashing down, like in a forest. He and She were on opposite sides of it. They froze in place and looked at each other across it, the whole stage dimmed when it crashed except for the spotlights on them like at the beginning, and He and She were in the same places that they had started at, the spotlights hadn't moved. They looked at each other in silence for a long, long time, their last words still hanging in the air, behind the sound of the crash of the tree, if you know what I mean. Curtain.

I don't know, you had to be there, she says. The play was great, the words. And the sex that night was amazing.

Talk to young people and they say that's what's missing, spiritual community, Jeon says. Community means something different now, they say, because it's all self-selecting, right? To find out what church is all about, you don't go to a church, you look it up online in twenty minutes. No seeking, just search, you feel me? What's going to happen when this generation hits middle age, the time of ceasing to choose and starting to live within your choices? You follow me? If that's what middle age is. Maybe their kind of community won't close down in the same way, you know what I mean? The older hipsters?

You understand what I'm saying?

What it is that I'm trying to say, is that—

You get what I'm saying?

You see what I'm getting at?

You follow?

JULY 9, 2016   SATURDAY

Six more women come forward to accuse Roger Ailes of sexual harassment.

My glance strays vaguely through the newspaper and I read these lines:

Co-op feuds may be as common in New York as shouting matches between cabbies, but at 25 Tudor City Place, part of a petite neighborhood of 11 apartment buildings and four brownstones with an Old English look, the jousting has turned particularly fervent. Two weeks ago, residents elected three new board members and effectively ousted two incumbents after a bitter war waged with reams of leaflets and letters.

Tudor City is set apart from the street grid. East 41st and 43rd Streets end in cul-de-sacs, forcing traffic to go around, and East 42nd passes under a bridge. There are also four shaded parks; two of them are technically private, but open to the public—unlike Gramercy. Most of the neighborhood, which takes up six blocks, has landmark status, though newer apartments, like the Hamilton, a 21-story brown-brick co-op on East 40th Street, loom on the edges.

I've been to Tudor City once. Does it mean anything that the United Nations is on the site of old slaughterhouses? You can see it from Tudor City, but only if you're outside—they didn't put in windows facing the river when they built the apartment buildings, to avoid the stench. Another of New York's strange enclaves, a ye olde towne with shingles outside the small ground-floor mom-and-pop shoppes; stained-glass windows in the faux-gothic stone façade of the restaurant (pub); two little parks that remind me of the plots of simples and medicinals at the Cloisters: orderly, medieval, microcosmic, useful. The old people walking their dogs and the very old people sitting on the benches don't know each other, but get to before my eyes: "Oh, 15C? When did you move in? Early '80s?"

JULY 10, 2016   SUNDAY

I'd stayed up late in San Francisco reading about *Dead Man* and then about the Orlando shooting. I went to bed in the melancholy yet gentle hours of approaching day. The whole afternoon was off. I heard the music of *Dead Man* running through my head, those long, piercing guitar notes that mean Western, in the Neil Young whine-tone, with some railroad-wheel chunka-chunka, heavy reverb and palm-muted low strings. Mostly it's a haunting modal melody, flexible, major-minor, never resolving, drowning in Neil Young emotion.

Young has nothing obvious to do with Blake, the voracious reader and annotator, the creator of intricate, densely worked mythologies. But something links them together in my mind. The early, pre-prophetic Blake of *Songs of Innocence and Experience* tunnels straight to an emotional, psychological core like some of Young's songs. And there is something about sons. A Japanese novel with a title from Blake, almost an autobiography—*Rouse Up O Young Men of the New Age!*—is about a writer whose whole creative life, whole way of living in the world, has been inspired by Blake and by his, the writer's, severely disabled son. Neil Young, too, has a son with severe cerebral palsy, probably the most important person in his life; Young calls him his spiritual guide. O Young Men.

I decided to find the soundtrack album. Around the corner from the hotel was the record store I used to go to back when I used to go to the Empire Theater. They had it on CD, and my laptop could play it.

He recorded the soundtrack alone in a warehouse, with the two-and-a-half hour rough cut of the movie playing straight through and Neil on his guitar, sometimes organ, two or three times straight through refusing to stop the film during the recording and then done. As though the film were the visualtrack to the concert;—the music as sound *track,* running parallel the whole length of the trip. Young sent Jarmusch the demos to give him a sense of his ideas, and Jarmusch said they had to use them like that, improvised alongside and all. Meanwhile, Jarmusch says in the liner notes, he had written the movie in the first place listening to Neil Young constantly, and filmed it listening to him, and took the crew to a Young concert during the shoot, and the editor had even been able to cut a few sequences of the film to existing Young instrumentals to try to woo him for the project. It is impossible to say how much of the movie is Young's, Jarmusch says. The CD has more dialogue and sound effects from the movie than most other soundtrack CDs; someone on the internet called it a "composer's cut" of the movie.

Young has an inner force, a propulsion, moving him here or there—he has to not let thought, his or others', get in the way or impede that movement. Like what he says about sound engineering: start with a good signal and don't put anything in the line. He has a volume pedal that works by moving a remote little robot arm that physically turns the volume knob on the amp, so as not to put anything between guitar and amp that could slow up the signal. Keep The Line Clear—it's a hippie idea. It privileges authenticity over any standards of quality, but I'm not sure Young has ever made ugly music—dippy, bombastic, puerile, but not ugly.

The liner notes had photos of Young, animalistic, totemic, hunched over his guitar in front of the film in a big bare room. I decided I needed to see the studio. "Recorded at Mason St. Studios, S.F., CA" it said on the back of the CD booklet.

I couldn't find a website for the place—it must have shut down or changed names in the nineties, a couple years before the internet. No hits at all on Google except for one obscure page that transcribed the liner notes I already had. I looked all along Mason Street on Google Earth for studios with other names—nothing. Eventually I gave up on the internet and went to the San Francisco Public Library to pageview phonebooks from the early to mid '90s. There was a building to enter, a floor to find, stairs to take, a shelf to bend down to, heavy books to carry to a free seat at one of the tables among the other people there and discarded books in that spongy green library hardcover—perhaps you remember these hurdles from the analog days, dear reader, it probably depends how old you are.

When he was visiting family in Florida recently, Ben said, and had to mail something, he'd asked two eighteen-year-olds at the mall where he could find a mailbox: "A what?" the first said. He tried to explain. "What do you mean?" the first said. "Oh, like one of those big blue things?" her friend said.

In a 1993 white pages I find it, Mason St. Studios, 540 Hampshire St. From there I could find the cross-street on the internet, I'll give it that. I was tired—I'd go see it tomorrow, my last day in San Francisco, Father's Day.

JULY 11, 2016   MONDAY

Donald Trump, the real estate mogul and reality television star who has taken center stage in the race for the Republican presidential nomination this week, delivered a rambling monologue in Phoenix, Arizona, introduced by Sheriff Joe Arpaio of Maricopa County, whose tactics in tracking down illegal immigrants drew national attention and a federal ruling against him for racial profiling in 2013.

The speech was hosted by the Republican Party of Maricopa County and drew several thousand people to the Phoenix Convention Center. It had a distinctly celebratory air as Mr. Trump lauded the "massive" crowds he has drawn and the attention he has brought to immigration and other issues that he said "weak" politicians were afraid to address. "I went to the Wharton School of Business," he also noted several times. "I'm, like, a really smart person."

"The silent majority is back, and we're going to take our country back," Mr. Trump declared as he left the stage.

Arizona's senators, John McCain and Jeff Flake, both Republicans, decided not to attend the event, as did the Republican governor, Doug Ducey. For many here, the event revived an image of the state, embodied by Sheriff Arpaio, as unwelcoming and harsh in its enforcement of illegal immigration laws—a perception that Mr. Ducey has worked hard to dispel.

At around 6:00 a.m., 41-year-old Jason Brooks was standing naked with multiple guns at the intersection of 16th and Gaty Avenue in East St. Louis, Illinois, shooting at bystanders, homes, and passing cars. When he fired in the direction of two officers, they returned fire, killing him.

Theresa May has won the leadership contest of the Conservative Party in the United Kingdom and will be the next Prime Minister.

I have heard conjectures that it may be as painful to be born as to die. I think it probable, Josh quotes.

JULY 12, 2016   TUESDAY

Donald Trump claimed that after the killing of police officers in Dallas, political-correctness-minded people were "calling for a moment of silence" for the killer. This did not happen.

I spent a long day walking in the mountains this weekend, Iris told us yesterday, roads snaking around the middles of hillsides. High vertical rocks on the other sides of ravines, with tufts of green on the top, a very Chinese effect, or else overlooking big river-valleys, one jolly blue lake close by and others in the farther, hazier distances. The peaks were surprisingly jagged for there to be so many of them tumbled all across the horizon. There was a small, postcard-perfect waterfall in a high valley, a wide sheet of white ending in a calm pool of green, and only at the end of the day was there one that was more sublime, thin forking paths of white lightning down a high dark rock face. The first one hissed, the second one rumbled. Yellow and black lizards, motionless on the ground like thrown-out candy bar wrappers, suddenly moved and were visible as what they were: moved so fast that they seemed to reappear an inch or two farther down the path, angled left instead of right, without passing through the space between.

I watch a talk online, at home with a swollen foot:

The reason any day that starts off on the internet is a bad day is "decision fatigue," the speaker says. It turns out our brains have only so much decision-making oomph and once we use it up for the day we get all crabby, make bad choices, snap judgments, careless and irresponsible decisions—sound familiar? (the audience laughs offscreen)—until we recharge by going to sleep.

They haven't found anything but sleep that can replenish our choosing.

This, then, the speaker says, is the answer to the riddle of the ages: What Is Sleep? A cool, restorative recrystallization of our ability to decide. But I digress. Decision fatigue is why car salesmen ask you to make all kinds of pointless decisions first—cupholder? power windows? upholstery fabric?—so that half an hour later you give up and go along with the expensive options they suggest.

The web is, obviously to everyone, a huge waste of time, among all the other things it is, but that's not enough to explain why it ruins the rest of your day. Even for the disciplined—get online, scan the feed and the inbox, read the important ones, answer the vital ones, click it closed bam boom, no links no news no magazines no Twitter no YouTube, even I manage it sometimes (the audience laughs offscreen)—it's less than five minutes, not enough time to ruin anything, but it ruins the day anyway. Because every single thing is something you *could* pay attention to, so that even if you've resisted you have had to decide to resist. The web is a trillion decisions mainlined right into your gently beating heart: automatic decision fatigue.

The opposite isn't doing nothing, it's something like a well-designed park, and the speaker got to the point of his talk. Frederick Law Olmsted understood the problem. He specifically intended the wide, gently sweeping paths of Central Park and his other designs to give strollers as little as possible to have to decide about: where to go, how to avoid oncoming people, what destination to head toward. He knew that the restorative psychological effects he was going for were undercut and betrayed by conscious decisions, even conscious attention, to grand views, special plantings, noticeable sights or sounds or smells of any kind.

Olmsted learned on a ramble through England that the beautiful can never have clearly defined edges or limits—it has to fade into the hazy, mysterious distance. He preferred the common wildflower modestly growing in the mossy turf to imported exotics blooming in an enameled vase under a glass bell. He didn't care what trees were called and didn't add labels for parkgoers to decide whether or not to look at.

I shut the tab and look out my other window, at the park outside, a lesser Olmsted. The seasons are changing, but I think I've described enough weather here—it Exemplifies Mutabilitie, that's probably all that needs to be said. I don't know how people used to experience weather but now it too is political. I remember clouds as unrepeatable mysteries, chasing each other across the world of the sky, not partisan evidence; I remember the heat and the cold, warned only by an analog thermometer nailed to the frame outside my living-room window. They're chopping down all the trees but at least they can't despoil the sky, people used to say, centuries ago.

JULY 13, 2016   WEDNESDAY

Mr. Chernow, a Pulitzer Prize winner whose *Alexander Hamilton* was a principal source for the Broadway musical *Hamilton,* said he had been struck by Mr. Trump's lack of reference to the founding documents of American history, or to presidents like George Washington, Abraham Lincoln and Franklin D. Roosevelt. "The only historical movement that Mr. Trump alludes to is a shameful one—'America First,'" Mr. Chernow said, referring to the isolationist political organization at the time Nazi Germany was taking power across Europe.

Theresa May has become Prime Minister. She has chosen chronically disheveled Boris Johnson as her Foreign Secretary.

The pain in my feet was too much and I took two of the white pills, not one, and a half of the blue pill, not a quarter, and together, not alternating. This time to dull the throbbing was not enough, to lie in bed with my feet up was not enough.

As they started to work I felt so grateful. The medicine is powerful to the point where it seems like magic. Here, here is what we have all always wanted—relief for the wounded, a balm to the wrathful, forgiveness to the guilty, forgetfulness for the resentful, understanding for the victimized falsely persecuted and sentenced. Oh subtle, just, and mighty opioids! I fell into a reverie on that summer night, at my open window. I sat from sunset to sunrise, motionless and not wishing to move.

From the room I could overlook the park a short distance below me and command a view of the great city beside and beyond it with its boxy projects, abandoned warehouses, and new glass and steel. Paths writhed and played, trees argued and reconciled. One cloud-clump of oak leaves turned to me and explained that this view was the world: The surrounding city is the striving of status and money—exhausted prosperity of trade, black and brown underclass, shining towers of finance capital—and in its midst is a space elsewhere. The turmoil and restless activity of the city and the calm tranquility of the park had traded places or meanings. Now it was the paths and trees in never-ceasing movement and life.

After a time the landscape faded from attention and there were people, armies, hordes, some holding medieval pikes and halberds and others with long nineteenth-century rifles, and they whirled and moved upon one another in a Trojan War of heroism, tragedy, and incident. The greatest epics of screen and song were as nothing compared to the staggering richness of detail before my eyes. The battle seethed for years.

To these people succeeded dreams of lakes and silvery expanses of water:—

For several reasons, I have not been able to compose the notes for this part of my narrative into any regular and connected shape. I give the notes disjointed as I find them, or have now drawn them up from memory. Much has been omitted.

JULY 14, 2016 THURSDAY

For some reason I remember the last record store I passed when I was walking on pain-free feet. Popwax, a neighborhood institution. Sells CDs too, plus the whole range of vinyl from nondescript to artisanal. There was a sign on the door, in blue marker, announcing their then-upcoming sale which must be nearly over now: 40% off all LPs and cassettes. The sign in the window said, the door announced: Analog Days.

There *are* sacred places, Edward told us at the bar recently. We all have them, our job is to find them. I was in the south of France once, near the Mediterranean, and there was a large pink house looking out over some Roman ruins. If you turn your back on the house and face away from the ruins too there is a loose grove of olive trees, sunk low, between walls that are low on this side and high on the other. Probably it would be truer to say that we were built up, not that it was sunk down. Now that grove is a park, with little soccer games tucked between the rows of trees.

A few years later I saw an old monastery, a monastic community that was now a school. It was summer, so looking over the wall I saw an empty schoolyard, where monks probably used to grow their food one or two thousand years ago. There were painted wooden animals on springs, playground structures at the far end, and a pair of waist-high soccer goals set up near me in a clearing between the wildflower snowdrifts against the old stone walls of the buildings. Something about those two white metal bars, each bent into three sides of a rectangle and rammed down into the dirt, facing each other across half a schoolyard empty of children, seemed more ancient than the monastic community, or Stonehenge, or the Pyramids.

I only remembered the olive grove later. The two places were less alike than I have made them sound—one northern, in the summer, the other southern, in spring; busy and empty; and so on. But who knows how these different things rhyme and what they speak to in us.

I asked Edward if he ever did figure out what it was about those places that so moved him, and he said no, he hadn't. Anne-Sofie only smiled her sarcastic smile—she had heard it all before.

A truck drove through a crowd of people who were celebrating Bastille Day on the Promenade des Anglais in Nice, France. The driver, a 31-year-old Tunisian man, was shot by police. 85 others dead.

"Soleil noir. Black sun."

"Black Star."

"Hey man, he got out while the going was good."

JULY 15, 2016   FRIDAY

The GOP nominee had initially planned to announce his running mate at a press conference at Trump Tower, but decided to postpone the event because of his "emotional reaction" to the atrocity in Nice, France, while continuing to hold fundraising events anyway and call into multiple news shows on Thursday night, not obviously emotional. He then announced his running mate on Twitter, ahead of the originally scheduled news conference time, unveiled a dirty joke of a logo, and news leaked that as of midnight on Thursday he had been asking his top aides how he could still back out of the decision. "Don Jr., friends say, is for Newt," according to reports. At his formal introduction of his running mate, he talked about himself, said he would get to Pence's qualifications in "just a minute," then talked for another twenty minutes, constantly being, according to the *New York Times,* pulled over to the subject of himself by a sort of a gravitational narcissistic pull that takes command whenever he attempts to utter a compound thought: "So one of the primary reasons I chose Mike was I looked at Indiana, and I won Indiana big," he said, for instance. After muttering "back to Mike Pence," he called him "a solid person," clapped him on the shoulder, and left the stage.

After I recovered from the opioids yesterday, my feet did feel better. I make it outside and buy flowers. A jostle of unopened pink tulips on a table in front of a window as the sunlight moves through the park outside.

Tonight the Turkish military launched a coordinated operation in several major cities to topple the government and unseat President Recep Tayyip Erdoğan.

Tanks rolled onto the streets of Istanbul; Turkish fighter jets dropped bombs on their own parliament, while Hulusi Akar, Chairman of the Joint Chiefs of Staff, was kidnapped by his own security squad. A statement read on state-owned TRT (Turkish Radio and Television), by a news anchor at gunpoint, said that the military had completely taken over the administration of the country to reinstate constitutional order, and a new constitution was in preparation. The statement accused the Erdoğan government of eroding democracy, announced a curfew, and imposed martial law across the country.

A few minutes later, Prime Minister Binali Yıldırım denounced the coup attempt on Twitter, and Erdoğan, speaking on FaceTime to a CNN Turk (Cable News Network, Turkey) anchor who held up her phone so viewers could see him, urged the public to take to the streets in protest. Thousands of ordinary citizens, armed with nothing more than kitchen utensils, gathered in streets and squares around Anatolia. The crowds resisted tank fire and air bombardments and, with the help of loyalist soldiers and police forces, defeated the coup attempt in a matter of hours; despite explosions at parliament buildings in Ankara, Interior Minister Efkan Ala soon announced that the coup attempt had been neutralized. Troops taking part surrendered at Taksim Square in Istanbul. 241 people killed, 2,194 injured.

The Turkish government immediately blamed the failed coup attempt on Fethullah Gulen, a Turkish preacher who has lived in self-imposed exile in the U.S.

since 1999. Around 6,000 people were swiftly detained and arrests will continue, according to Turkey's Foreign Ministry; dozens of media outlets were also shut down. Military officials, pilots, police officers, civil servants, academics, and teachers have been fired for alleged links to Gulen's movement; the total would soon rise to 100,000 people fired or suspended and 37,000 arrested, in an unprecedented crackdown.

The word *taksim*, Josh tells us, can mean to divide, to gather, or to channel water, which is why the great field then outside the city of Istanbul, which Nerval visited a dozen years before his death at age forty-six, where he saw cemeteries in the fields and vendors selling meatballs and watermelon, and which also served as a water distribution center, came to be known as Taksim.

JULY 16, 2016   SATURDAY

Trump's comments, as potential commander in chief, were, in their entirety: "So many friends in Turkey. Great people, amazing people. We wish them well. A lot of anguish last night, but hopefully it will all work out."

Senior military officials who spoke with the *New York Times*, responding to Donald Trump's speeches about finally getting serious in the war on terror (intentionally killing the family members of suspected terrorists; waterboarding: "I love it! I think it's great!") revealed alarm over many of Mr. Trump's proposals for the use of American power, even among officers who said privately that they lean Republican. "We remember the Nuremberg trials," said ret. Maj. Gen. Paul D. Eaton, the man in charge of training the Iraqi Army in 2003. "Just following orders is not going to cut it."

"To be clear about this: senior active-duty military officers are warning that a man who could become president might give orders that would expose them to war-crime prosecution later on. For time-capsule purposes, this is part of the public record just days before the Republican party officially makes this man its nominee, and three-and-a-half months before the country decides whether to make him Commander in Chief."

I am able to make it out to a talk at the NYPL, connected to its exhibit of geology and photography. That third-floor hall, always dimly lit, always nearly empty, archival photos that feel archival. For the talk they had a foreign writer with a thick unplaceable accent in his deep rich voice, and he talked about stones. I could have listened for hours.

Here is a ssstone from the park, he intones. I feel closer to thisss stone than to other people, more like it than like other people. I write for the stone, even though the stone won't read me, but let's be honest, how many people will either, out of all the people in the world, and the ones that do will read me in their own way, not necessarily my way of writing, any sense I have of having achieved some kind of connection or bond with them will be imagined on my part too. It's no different than the stones. I have never felt like I *belong* to the human *race* or sssomesssing. I am a part of nature, and in that sense I belong with the human race, which is also a part of nature. This iss why the photographss here speak to me. Do they speak to you? I belong with the schisssst, I belong with the gneissss. Other than that, no, I cannot take the side of this or that person. That is why I am a writer. A filmmaker has to feel close to people. Or a singer. Or a weaver. Not painters and not writers.

A sad looking older man in a bright white suit, in a motorized wheelchair—stubble, flicking the joystick to slide silently forward—pulls up to his friends, the group of famous people in the room, and breaks into what looks like a wry smile as he talks with them, catching up. Long, almost bushy eyebrows, tight Greek curls of white-gray hair, exquisite pale blue shirt that matches his eyes, a gaze like he's talking about at least fifteen years past. At one point, the most beautiful of the famous women tries to take off her jacket, and he, not her husband, helps her. He must be a filmmaker, or weaver.

JULY 17, 2016   SUNDAY

An ambush of Baton Rouge police officers has left 3 dead and 3 injured. While police nationwide and in the Louisiana city in particular have been on high alert after the killings of Alton Sterling and five police officers in

Dallas, a Missouri man identified as Gavin Eugene Long of Kansas City went on a shooting rampage that left two policemen and a sheriff's deputy dead, police sources said.

It was just around 8:30 a.m. on July 17, Long's 29th birthday. A white Chevrolet Malibu pulled up next to Matthew Gerald, a 41-year-old rookie Baton Rouge cop sitting in his patrol car at an Airline Highway red light. In the stolen white rental car were two semi-automatic rifles, a 9mm handgun, and a rambling suicide note that spoke of "horrendous acts of violence" and his growing rage toward the police.

The murder weapon was an AR-15 style semi-automatic rifle, law enforcement sources told CNN. Long, an African American former Marine, had served as a data network specialist, spent time in Iraq, received a Good Conduct Medal, Iraq Campaign Medal, and National Defense Service Medal, and was honorably discharged with the rank of sergeant in 2010. He was killed by a SWAT officer during the shootout with police at the scene.

540 Hampshire St. four Sundays ago was in part of the city that had changed—shiny corrugated shared workspaces and Berlinish cement-block cafés swarming round the low rows of wooden bungalows and old warehouses. It was a long low façade of gray horizontal wood in the morning light, with a triangle jutting up in the middle, like an Illuminati pyramid, or else the

peak of an A-frame, depending how mystical you were feeling. The doors were open, and inside were a couple guys moving equipment around—it was NYStudiosSF now, mostly for ads and corporate infotainment, and the guys hadn't heard of Mason St. Studios but they told me NYSSF had been there for fifteen, sixteen years, which was about right. Every now and then I could hear the sound of a train moving south from the edge of the city.

I asked if there was a big recording room in the place and they said there was one central space, a projector and some sound equipment could fit in there—yes, it would reverb and echo a lot. They took me in. Nothing, of course. Nothing I could recognize from the hunched grainy pictures, just a little stage and some chairs set up and some metal girders overhead that, if I tried, I could think looked like train tracks. The chairs were for a church group, the guys told me—they rented out the space on weekends to Canterbury Fellowship. I could come sit in on their Meeting at noon if I wanted. Now they had to get back to work . . .

They let me sit for a while, so I sat on the folding chairs, legs straight out and head back, looking up at the tracks. I imagined an atom or two of the guitar sound still echoing around the room—just an atom—bouncing up against my face, entering my skin.

The room slowly started to fill up, and I sat up straight in the chair and looked toward the front, not up at the ceiling. Before long it was packed, about three-quarters Mexican and Salvadoran, one quarter white. If

I'd seen the white people on the street I wouldn't have thought they were Canterburyers. The service alternated Spanish and English.

The pastor rose and in a mild voice of unassuming authority began.

Bienaventurado el varón que no anduvo en consejo de malos! Blessed is the man who walks not in the counsel of the wicked! For we are pilgrims all, my brothers and sisters, and none of us walks alone. We all have traveling companions, and woe unto you if you choose the bad one, reject the godly one. We all must accept the counsel of others to help us on our way, and let them be family and friends, the good and the just, not smugglers and coyotes. In this world, my friends, Sin that pays its way can travel freely, and without a passport; Virtue, if poor, is stopped at all borders.

The sermon went on, it ran something like the following but I do not pretend to quote:—

These are the very first words of the first Psalm, my friends, which is the book in the Bible where God, praised be his name, stops talking to us and instead lets us sing back praise from the godly place within us to Him. But listen, its wisdom is a warning. This verse, the beginning of the Psalms, tells us what we should not do, not what we should do. Blessed are those who walk *not* in the counsel of the wicked. Feel the beauty in this, my sisters and brothers, the loving kindness for us poor weak struggling hombres y mujeres. It starts by assuming we cannot even recognize the true path—all we know is the voice in our heart that tells us to resist the wicked counsel around us.

Note the poetry of the rest of the first verse: "Blessed is the man who walks not in the counsel of the wicked, Nor stands in the path of sinners, Nor sits in the seat of the scornful." The words themselves mark a path of darkness, the downward way, and lets us see that yea we can know it, and exhorts us to avoid it. This evil course is to walk, then stand, then sit. First taking the advice of, then being near, then staying among. The wicked, the sinners, the scornful.

Wicked in the Scripture is the most general contrast to righteous. The wicked, with their oh so abundant advice, may indeed be moral in their conduct toward their fellow-creatures, and outwardly unblameable, but they live without due regard to God, unsettled, aiming at no certain end. If we do follow their advice, we will meet open and notorious sinners, who may insnare us, drawing us by degrees into an imitation of their practices. If we do that, we may end by sitting in the company of the scornful, the most specific word of the three. Deliberate association with those who openly mock and scorn is the third step in this, the career of evil. We end up with them, at the end of this evil road, sitting, no longer traveling down any path at all.

That is what we must not do. Blessed are those who do not do these things, the Psalm says.

The Hebrew word for blessing here is *esher*, from a word that means to go straight, go forward, advance, set right. Yes, my friends, to go the right way is blessedness indeed. Spurred on by the counsel of the wicked, surrounded by sinners on the move, we must not tarry, nor give up hope of moving onward, not lose the will and heart to travel our own way, the righteous direction. Our fellowship is named Canterbury, brothers and sisters, a place known for its many very different pilgrims.

When we are blessed, that path is straight ahead; for you and me and the rest of us struggling to follow the Lord, that path will not be straight, it will have detours and backtracks and dead ends, but take heart! We are told that if we reject evil counsel and company, the squirming and winding path will have been straight and true. Who knows the geometry God's eye can see! With the walls and dark forces blocking our way, these twists and turns might be the straight path for us.

The pastor came by afterward to welcome me, a newcomer or visitor in his congregation, and I felt less out of place with him than I'd felt in a long time. He asked me about my path, the journey that had brought me to Canterbury, and I hinted at distant travels, never fulfilling; secret yearnings, always unexpressed. He shook my hand with his left hand on my shoulder and a smile in his eyes. His face no longer looked dry and gouged as though blasted by desert winds, it crinkled with kindness. He invited me to join him and the fellowship at their potluck lunch; I hadn't brought anything, I said, but he said that that was all right, I had brought myself.

I sat down next to her. It was her again, Sylvie. I knew it, my mind was racing, what should I do.

I listened to her talk to her friends at the table and waited until it was natural for me to jump in with a comment, addressed to the woman sitting across from her. When they asked me how I had come to Canterbury, I said nothing about Neil Young and something about being curious, interested in exploring the community and the faith here—that was the magic key, from then on they welcomed me in, encouraging and supportive and a little missionary.

I asked Sylvie about how she'd come to Canterbury, and she told me a story, entirely unembarrassed. The others had clearly heard it before, or had similar ones of their own.

She had taken a year off from college, her senior year, and was living with her boyfriend, two years older. He'd died of an overdose, heroin.

For a while she'd really lost her way. She never did finish college.

Then she'd met someone who told her about the First Spiritualist Church. I was skeptical at first, of course, she said. I thought it was just me needing to feel a connection with him again. But it was really him, from the Spirit World. The medium was amazing, he was so sensitive to the vibrations.

Mostly that he loved me, he wanted me to be happy. He understood what I was going through.

No, the messages aren't heard by outward manifestations.

It was a Message Circle. We sat in a ring of chairs, the lights were dimmed, there was a little table in the middle with a candle. It was a very safe psychically charged setting for receiving communications. We called them those who had crossed over, not the dead, the church doesn't actually communicate with someone who's dead, a person's spirit lives on in another dimension, the Spirit World. The spirit identifies himself through the medium, describing their personality or appearance or how they crossed over or other identifying characteristics, then they give a message, usually expressions of love, guidance, healing, gestures of help with your life, or regret or apologies for things they feel they did wrong.

The Message service proves that life continues after physical death. It is just as complete, actually more complete, in the next plane.

We never die.

I left that church when I moved out here, none of the branches here seemed right for me, and I didn't need to hear from him so much anymore. I know now that he is always with me. I can follow my own path, like we heard today.

Some of them always went out for coffee after the lunch and final benediction, and they invited me to join them.

I didn't tell Sylvie we knew each other or ask her the questions that would have proven it. I didn't need proof, I knew. She was going by another name now, that was fine.

I gently brought up New York, where she said she had never been—she must have decided to forget about that part of her life. I would need to respect that, not bring it up again. But she said was going to New York for the first time next month.

I told her I lived there and waited for the right time to give her my email and offer to show her around.

JULY 18, 2016   MONDAY

Tony Schwartz, who wrote Donald Trump's *The Art of the Deal* and knows him probably better than anyone, considers him a sociopath, the *New Yorker* reported today.

DANGEROUSLY HOT TEMPERATURES EXPECTED THIS WEEK AS MASSIVE HEAT DOME ENVELOPS MUCH OF U.S.

So far this summer, there have been a couple of high-pressure ridges aloft (bulges in the jet stream) that have prevailed across the U.S. One ridge was positioned around the

Western U.S., and the other was in the Southeast. As this week progresses, we will see a bridging of these ridges resulting in one massive dome of high pressure. Beneath this dome, air sinks and warms, resulting in hot temperatures. Under these conditions, thunderstorm activity will become sporadic, so many areas will be dry.

In addition to the hot temperatures, heat indices—a measure of how hot it feels—will be dangerously high with values in the 110- to 100-degree range in some locations.

Whenever it's not too far out of my way I try to walk past the Marble Cemetery on 2nd Street. It is the quietest place I know, like a portrait of Silence the god of silence, a frieze. I have never seen anyone in it, not a squirrel, a bird, any other animal; the long, long fence on the street side is always locked and the back windows of the four- or five-story tenement buildings on the other side look down in stillness on stillness. Of all the places in New York City to dream you could live, those buildings on East 3rd are the ones that feel most like real dreams—unconscious, vivid, impossible to remember. It is strange to imagine not the inside of an apartment or the front of a building but only a window or two in the back,—not even sitting by the window looking out, but the window, the glass.

There are few gravestones, far apart from one another; the long, thin shape uses up the maximum possible prime street-facing real estate, a fact which itself must be a sign of the cemetery's age. The plaque on the fence does little to explain the place, who is buried there and why, aside from the fact that they're dead. I still remember a children's book with a quiet graveyard in an enclosure—spaces within spaces, enclosers enclosed—it must be an image that does something for me.

(The exception could be parts of the Northeast, especially New England, where this pattern sometimes allows cold fronts to back into the area from the northeast. Thunderstorms and somewhat cooler temperatures can result.)

I am standing at the fence looking in, and it is so quiet I don't notice the first few raindrops, but soon it's coming down in sheets, then in masses even more solid. Without thinking I try to find shelter.

At the end of the block is the Film Archive, and a sign in the lobby is advertising a special screening not listed in the calendar or on the website. Because of the politically sensitive nature of the movie, smuggled out of the filmmaker's repressive country, it was decided to show it without advertising it on the internet in any way. I had never heard of the filmmaker; the movie was about to start. Only four or five other people were sitting in the theater, far apart from each other. The likeness to the Marble Cemetery struck me for the first time. The lights went down and it started.

Epigraph: and it stayed onscreen long enough to reread several times:

Your late arrival, my son, has caused me to devote a great deal of time, spent in continual nightly vigils, to reveal in writing & to leave behind to you as a memory, after my own physical demise, & for the common benefit of mankind, such knowledge as God has granted me thanks to the revolutions of the stars.

—Nostradamus

The credit sequence was stolen from some French New Wave movie I didn't recognize—sans-serif bold white names on a black background, all Véroniques and Jean-Pierres and Phillippes and Laurents. They left off the régisseur and actors, gave just the minor credits: Montage followed by some French name, it said. Maquillage. Scriptgirl, Image, Son.

They're gone, the voiceover begins over ordinary images, the camera rambling around a room. He was curious and interested enough, getting snapped into the car seat, milk and blueberries, then I leaned down to kiss his beautiful, beautiful head and say Bye, have a good trip with Mama, I love you, I'll miss you, bye-bye and he started howling and I shut the car door and went back upstairs. He will have soon stopped: the verb tense of absence, future-past-future-imaginary.

Now I can begin my "effort." Not a film—let me make that clear as can be to anyone watching this! Dear censor, dear prosecutor, dear torturer! I am well aware of and fully and zealously compliant with the government ban on my "filming, producing theater, writing novels, or storytelling in any other form whatsoever"!

My sentence has been read out to me and I accept it, as it already says on the form I signed in the interrogation room as best I could before the handcuffs were taken off.

With my family away I plan to take a few private notes on the film I had hoped to make and now never will. This document, then, dear censor, is mere notes on notes, a diary of a diary, about an unmade film about a country that is not yours—not Myanmar, not Tibet, not Russia, not North Korea . . . The movie, as I'm sure you know, was to be called *The Salt Smugglers*, my seventeenth film, about a band of outsiders and their crushing life on the margins of our (not your!) nation. My "effort" is nothing of the sort. I am filming nothing, just taking a few videos on my phone for personal use; there are no images of our vast western salt plains, the white hills raked into grids and quincunxes, lunar horizons of bare and blinding immensity, just some modest moments in my modest house; there are no soundscapes of windstorms crossing the plains, clanking fixtures on the primitive carts, carpets beaten free of the salt trodden into them downwind from the smuggler's tents, just some coffee being made, a few conversations, the noise of a little of my humble work. Since it just so happens that my wife is visiting her parents with our son today, my effort, though private in any case, will contravene neither our fine law that images of women even in their homes must be veiled, the realism of the character's behavior rightly and nobly made subordinate to the fact of the actress's images in the public sphere—nor the admittedly pettier concerns of artistic truth. Not that my little effort can legally or possibly claim to be art, dear functionary.

To begin.

It is a strange feeling, putting L into the car and watching him drive away. I have never been apart from my son like this, not since the moment he was born and I went with him and the nurse into the other room to clean him and weigh him and count his fingers (10) and toes (10) while the doctors sewed Mama up. Now he leaves and howls again and I think about my greatest fear, something happening to him, could I go on? This is for him, then, whether he wants it or not doesn't matter—everything is for him. Not for you, justice minister!

So thinks, perhaps, the salt-smuggler N. in his tent on the western marshes. I am trying to imagine his life, merely daydreaming, certainly not writing interdicted memoir or story. I myself have been parted from my son, who is not named L, many times, as you know, most recently during my two months in prison.

I lay down tape to block out the scene that will never be filmed, when the smuggler comes back to his yurt or grass hut and shakes off the Himalayan snow or monsoon rain and the smuggler's wife is there—in words her face can go unmentioned, so here she is, in her veiled or unveiled glory. This would be the exposition, discussion of the competing band of smugglers and their schemes, introduction of the baby boy who would have played such a central motivating role in the putative plot, the smugglers' love and stoic silence. The family has one scrawny cow and a young calf, whose fate, and the mother cow's inarticulate response to it, mirrors and expresses much that the family itself suppresses.

Here, where I have my coffee table, is the central stove where the wife squats, boiling butter tea or mint tea or Turkish coffee. He enters from there, where the TV is, to accommodate the lights and the film camera and dolly on this side of the room. The camera doesn't cut back and forth between the speakers of the dialogue, as viewers expect, but tracks left and right, in a swinging kind of motion, purely horizontal but slow-fast-slow like a pendulum. This technique saves film and editing time, and is more natural for the actors, and most importantly gives a suspense to the conversation without the use of artificial background music. I am trying to decide, in a way, how much of the pleasure I get is from the finished movie (that will never be) and how much from the hard floor under my hands and knees and the ripping sound of the masking tape coming off of its roll and turning into a line there.

I move the armchair to lay down the mark where the boy would sit, motionless, entering and leaving the frame of the shot, paying attention. It is vital—I say this for the benefit of any budding government filmmakers, since I have no plans for this effort to ever reach any viewers in countries more open to art—it is vital to have, in every scene, a silent, third presence: someone watching, someone the viewer can occasionally identify with and remember to look at while the dialogue remains in play and open to both parties. If there are two figures in a scene, the viewer takes a side—alternately, tentatively, doesn't matter—but a third figure diverts that impulse and somehow both draws the viewer in and leaves him outside the lines of force between the other two. When there can't be a third person there, for plot reasons, use a window, a mirror, a TV, a portrait, or a pet. These are the only five alternatives. Strangely, it makes no difference if the third figure is looking at the other two, or if one or both of the others are looking at the, say, window—I'm not sure why that is. There is just enough room behind the sofa to shove the armchair, lay down tape, step back to check the angles, take a few pics on my phone (not a film, as we know! notes on notes . . .), and start pulling the tape up again.

JULY 19, 2016   TUESDAY

Day One of the Republican National Convention was yesterday, with vicious speeches from Mike Flynn, Jeff Sessions, Scott Baio, a grieving mother of a Benghazi casualty, and "Melania Trump." Today's speakers will include Mitch McConnell and Paul Ryan, Ben Carson and Chris Christie, Don Jr., and, says the Party, "lovely pro-golfer Natalie Gulbis, Mr. Trump's youngest daughter Tiffany, and Kerry Woolard, the General Manager of Trump Winery." Big-time winners all. To highlight Mr. Trump's charitable instinct, reveal his loving and doting side, and demonstrate his incredible business acumen, respectively.

Mark Slope finds it all gripping. What a magnificent story I could tell if I went online! he cries. Descriptions based on image searches; personal and historical background; the entire religious, social, linguistic, environmental, gastronomical, psychological, anthropological, tribal, physiognomic, spiritual, and fashion profiles of the various parties, their extended families, &c. There are limits to the libraries, even here in New York, anyway I try my best but researchers are made not born.

Fox News's biggest star, Megyn Kelly, has told investigators that Roger Ailes sexually harassed her about ten years ago when she was a young reporter, and so Ailes is out. He will be punished for decades of sadistic harassment and abuse by being given forty million dollars.

There is, in fact, a long history of smuggling salt in our land. It is the sign of an advanced political system, you might say, since every community in a state of nature has had ways to supply itself with the salt necessary for life; smugglers come into being only with borders, taxes, and/or wars. In our case it is taxes, or rather a law that mandates salt be purchased only from government agents (at prices they set), as a way for the government to raise revenue that is not technically tax, and to create lucrative posts that can be granted to loyal functionaries.

The smugglers in our case do not cross national borders, or not necessarily—they are more like black-marketeers, even, you might say, counterfeiters, trading in unauthorized currency. Fierce punishments await these enemies of the state, usually beheading. Their lives are bitter and cruel.

And so it goes on. The film is dubbed into accent-free English, and we never see the filmmaker's face, or his family—we see his hands, always in gloves. His house must have clues, but they're too subtle for me—the furniture, concrete walls, wood floors could be pretty much anywhere. I don't see any language, the spines on any of the books. The TV is on but staticky with a horizontal line moving continually up the screen then up the screen again from the bottom, the audio is white noise.

The filmmaker skips back and forth between different cultures, to avoid political persecution, of course, but the result, intended or not, is to privilege the imagination. As though salt is the freedom of the mind, crystalline, worldwide, now here now there.

I suppose there is no way to know for sure that the whole movie wasn't made right here in the U.S., in New York, in some rent-controlled loft around the corner, a conceptual MFA project or hoax of some sort. Some twenty-six-year-old kid trying to cash in on an unnamed dictatorship's political cred, or our longing to see dictatorships everywhere but here. Cash in in a loose sense, I mean, this isn't a commercial film and the kid couldn't ever claim it on a CV. So they would be using this unearned political cred for what, exactly?

The voiceover tells the story of *The Salt-Smugglers*: how a lord in the enemy camp is arrested and thrown in jail on the pretext that he is the leader of a rebel band of salt-smugglers. As he calmly, conclusively proves that he could not have taken part in the crimes of which he is accused, he realizes that no facts will be allowed to get in the way of this pretext, and amiably marches off to his jail cell. He escapes; is recaptured; then a major assault is launched on the prison and he and the others are freed—by, it turns out, the band of salt-smugglers and their real leader. At a roisterous tavern, the lord hears from the robber-king the people's grievances and the true reasons for the salt-smugglers' resistance. The lie turns true and the lord joins the band of outlaws. It is, of course, a folk-tale—at least with folk-tale elements: Robin Hood, etc.,—but in this telling the realism, not the legend, shines through the historical period-detail. If anything, the story seems to refer to the present. But the filmmaker has made sure not to make any detail too clear an allegory of anything: There is no fractious aristocracy in his country, he points out to his listeners in the government, no recent dramatic jailbreaks, no king in the salt-smuggler's tale remotely like the leader of the filmmaker's country. It feels allegorical without the allegory, which gives the story a strange kind of power and suspense, suspension, as he goes on to tell about the lord's further adventures, disguises, narrow escapes, pitched battles, clever ruses, heroic single combats, apparent setbacks, eventual triumphs.

Following the example of the fakirs and dervishes, he wandered the world, hoping to provide an example of humility and austerity. He called himself *The Dead Man*,—and it was under this name that he established a free school in the mid-sized city to the northwest.

I'm not old, but I don't think I'll live long, the filmmaker says after a pause. I've smoked my whole life; I've recently started to feel my heart in my chest, straining and gulping, pounding at unexpected times with a wet, sloppy sound I can feel. My joints don't yet ache, quite, but feel somehow near the end, like they are about to run down. My mind goes blank when I'm asked to say, or when I try on my own to say, what I'll be doing in ten years, or five, or two. I love everything about my son, everything, but all as fact, none as potential.

My work has all been of other people—not about, of. Other men and women before the camera, other characters' stories. When I'm gone, what will not-L have left of me? Memories, if I last long enough, if the government waits long enough before bringing me in one last time. Some family photos, which will probably seem like me to him even though they never seem like me to me—at most one or two do from when I was younger, but not the recent ones, not the ones with him. I cannot bring myself to believe that they are capable of supplying anything of me. He will have my films, records of my sensibility, but that will not be what he wants, he will want me as object, not seeing subject. I am starting to feel that I owe it to him to make a self-portrait.

But my art of other people would not be what it is if I felt comfortable with self-portraits. Maybe this is as close as I can get: showing me at work at showing.

Raking salt is a good way through the element of water: you skim the surface but don't mind bringing some water along; you make a pile of what you're drying but a wet pile, but that's okay, the sun and the air will dry the mound of salt as they wouldn't the salt still sitting on the surface of the lake. At the climax of one of my earlier films, of one of my films I should say, I had the hero say, as I used to think myself, that water defeated all things, everything succumbs to the horizontal in the end—but maybe, after all, even after everything and everything, not. We don't need to fight the impossible battle against what flows and seeps. All we need to do is let the salt support its own salt, hold its fellow crystals a foot or two off the surface, and everything will happen naturally. "It doesn't depend on efficiency in this work," the saltmen of Tibet sing while they rake. "It depends on the karma!"

At around this point the filmmaker made himself lunch, a long wordless scene that turned out to be my favorite in the movie. It was simple food, the kind a man makes to eat by himself, but he knew his way around the kitchen—he hadn't had someone to make him meals his whole life. He must have married late, the boy's age would fit that theory, assuming he didn't have grown sons already too, or maybe he had spent a lot of his time traveling alone, for his work, his art. Maybe men did the cooking in whatever country he was from—unlikely, but possible. His head remained out of the shot but we could see his body. With the camera artlessly set up on a tripod, static, he often left the frame to fetch or prepare something elsewhere in the kitchen, and we heard the sounds and watched time passing on the tiles behind the sink or the tomatoes on the counter. There was time for the mind to wander.

JULY 20, 2016   WEDNESDAY

Sylvie is coming from San Francisco to New York today. She gets in at six o'clock. I will see her again, take her out to dinner and look across the table into her deep gray eyes and hear her call me the nickname only she can use.

She will ask me what is wrong with my foot—the first one is nearly healed, the second is still bandaged up. I will tell her it's a long story.

On the train, people will be flickering in the brightly lit windows. We will must have been moving too fast for the I-beams holding up the subway tunnel to be visible directly, but we will have seemed to be sliding slowly ahead, slipping less slowly behind, then ahead again. In the other train, faces and torsos will sit and listen, sit and stare, the faces of the ones looking back visible from our forward-facing seats.

I will take her to the reopened Windows on the World in the new World Trade Center, "Cosmo and Damian" as the towers are affectionately known, I will tell her, the restaurant is in Damian. Was I in New York for the Christo project when he wrapped them in yellow so that they looked like two titanic sticks of butter standing on end, she will ask? I was.

I will think about children. In *Dead Man*, where are the children? There is one rocked in a cradle in Machine; Blake's Indian friend is kidnapped and sent to England as a child, where he discovers Blake's poetry; the shot faun is seen from overhead curled on the ground. Few women aside from Thel, but it doesn't feel like a masculine movie, the feminine is there, with cooking and nursing, the cross-dressing trapper, his hair care. Wm. Blake the original not the least feminine of poets. Death comes through the woman: the bullet through Thel.

Blue flowers are out on the High Line today, I hear. Butterfly bush. Foxglove: large clumps of purple vessels, unbroken. Amaranth the never-fading.

Coffee House Press began as a small letterpress operation in 1972 and has grown into an internationally renowned nonprofit publisher of literary fiction, essay, poetry, and other work that doesn't fit neatly into genre categories.

LITERATURE
is not the same thing as
PUBLISHING

Funder Acknowledgments

Coffee House Press is an internationally renowned independent book publisher and arts nonprofit based in Minneapolis, MN; through its literary publications, Coffee House acts as a catalyst and connector—between authors and readers, ideas and resources, creativity and community, inspiration and action.

Coffee House Press books are made possible through the generous support of grants and donations from corporations, state and federal grant programs, family foundations, and the many individuals who believe in the transformational power of literature. This activity is made possible by the voters of Minnesota through a Minnesota State Arts Board Operating Support grant, thanks to the legislative appropriation from the Arts and Cultural Heritage Fund. Coffee House also receives major operating support from the Amazon Literary Partnership, McKnight Foundation, and the National Endowment for the Arts (NEA). To find out more about how NEA grants impact individuals and communities, visit www.arts.gov.

Coffee House Press receives additional support from Bookmobile; the Buckley Charitable Fund; Dorsey & Whitney LLP; and the Schwab Charitable Fund.

The Publisher's Circle of Coffee House Press

Publisher's Circle members make significant contributions to Coffee House Press's annual giving campaign. Understanding that a strong financial base is necessary for the press to meet the challenges and opportunities that arise each year, this group plays a crucial part in the success of Coffee House's mission.

Recent Publisher's Circle members include many anonymous donors, Patricia A. Beithon, Robin Chemers Neustein, Kelli Cloutier, Theodore Cornwell, Jane Dalrymple-Hollo, Jeremy M. Davies, Mary Ebert and Paul Stembler, Kamilah Foreman, Eva Galiber, Bryan Garrett, Roger Hale and Nor Hall, William Hardacker, Randy Hartten and Ron Lotz, Carl and Heidi Horsch, Amy L. Hubbard and Geoffrey J. Kehoe Fund of the St. Paul & Minnesota Foundation, Hyde Family Charitable Fund, Kenneth & Susan Kahn, the Kenneth Koch Literary Estate, Cinda Kornblum, the Lenfestey Family Foundation, Carol and Aaron Mack, Gillian McCain, Mary and Malcolm McDermid, Daniel N. Smith III and Maureen Millea Smith, Vance Opperman, Mr. Pancks' Fund in memory of Graham Kimpton, Alan Polsky, Robin Preble, Ronald Restrepo and Candace S. Baggett, Elizabeth Schnieders, Steve Smith, Jeffrey Sugerman and Sarah Schultz, Paul Thissen, Allyson Tucker, Grant Wood, Margaret Wurtele, Aptara Inc., The Buckley Charitable Fund, Dorsey and Whitney Foundation.

For more information about the Publisher's Circle and other ways to support Coffee House Press books, authors, and activities, please visit www.coffeehousepress.org/pages/donate or contact us at info@coffeehousepress.org.

DAMION SEARLS is a renowned translator of the fiction of Nobel laureate Jon Fosse and dozens of other modern classics from German, French, Norwegian, and Dutch. A Guggenheim, Cullman Center, and two-time NEA fellow, he is the author of *The Inkblots* and *The Philosophy of Translation*.

Analog Days was designed by
Bookmobile Design & Digital Publisher Services.
Text is set in Adobe Caslon Pro.